Last Light Breaking

for Ann and the family

Patrick Corcoran

Last Light Breaking

seren

seren is the book imprint of
Poetry Wales Press Ltd
Wyndham Street, Bridgend, CF31 1EF, Wales

ISBN 1-85411-229-5

A Cataloguing in Publication record for this title
is available from the British Library

*The publisher works with the financial support of the
Arts Council of Wales*

Cover design: Simon Hicks. Photograph: Patrick Corcoran

Printed in Plantin by Creative Print and Design Wales, Ebbw Vale

I am old. I am old. I sit in my pyjama trousers, cold. It is evening. My curtains are not drawn. Before the bedroom window, huddled and hugging myself, I stare out over a city that does not know me.

"Not in bed, Pop... Here... Stop muttering to yourself and drink this tea. Look. I've brought some nice digestives." Noreen, my daughter-in-law, smiles in my direction without meeting my eyes. Places a cup beside me. Spilt tea has already softened the biscuits in the saucer. She goes downstairs again, to sit with my son. It was good of them to take me in.

My bedroom window is where I watch. Where I share in the street life outside. Where all I see clearly is the past. My image, reflected there, stares back, peers over my shoulder into the room behind me. I find it hard to accept that myopic, shrunken creature is me. I tilt weakly to the left, like a rootless Christmas tree, illuminated by the distant city lights. All festivities over. Discarded. Brittle pine needles would drop from my arms and legs, if someone were to brush past me.

I try to read the South Wales Echo but I am drawn back to examining my appearance. This is really me? Above frost-bitten ears my skin stretches taught, strains to contain my skull. Pale grey eyes reflect helplessness. Eyes which water in the cold air. Not just because the air is cold. Eyes which water when memories of Mammy return, Mammy who was not my mother but my wife. Eyes which fill with tears of hideous self-pity; to think that I am here, here alone, Mammy gone, and the world carries on as if nothing has happened.

I hear the floorboard creak just outside my room, "Pop, you've not touched your tea. It's stone cold. Your biscuits have gone soggy in the saucer again."

"So they have, Noreen, so they have." It is best not to argue about things like that with Noreen. She has a powerful left hook.

5

Broke the little finger in her left hand on the kitchen door one day, taking a swipe at Sean because he got home late and she had been worrying about him. "And you know something, Noreen? You won't believe this... I've a thirst on me I wouldn't sell for a quid."

"You'd better drink it then. I haven't got all night."

"Sláinte, girl. Sláinte... and may all yous troubles be little ones."

Noreen stands over me silently, waiting for the cup.

I hand her the cup with a slightly trembling hand. Noreen delivers a swift valediction, "It's well past your bedtime now, Pop. Don't forget you've got a busy day ahead tomorrow. Do be sensible."

"I will Noreen, dear. May God bless you and keep you safe." I listen to Noreen's footsteps retreat along the landing with what sounds to me an irritable haste. She is a fine woman. Cecil made an admirable choice. She has been the making of him.

Stiff from sitting, I edge crabwise to the bed. I pour water from the jug into the china bowl and freshen my face. The teeth go in to soak with some Steradent. Sans eyes, sans teeth, not quite sans everything. I do not think so.

My legs are milk white, almost transparent in the light, with purple patches where my veins have given up the ghost. I switch off the bedside lamp. Darkness. But I know where I am, who I am; not quite sans everything, no, no, not yet.

Tonight there will be no sweating, searching in a panic for Mammy, for a glimmer of light, for some memory or sign of which darkness I am in. I shall sleep soundly.

I am warm. No dreams to worry me. Cosy. I feel fifty years younger. I picture the old stone house in Bagenalstown. We are preparing to go out to Sunday Mass. A warm, summer's morning. Seven of us, all boys, in our best, chafing suits. We take no breakfast. We will be receiving Holy Communion and have to have abstained from all food and drink from midnight. The Parish Priest, Father Michael, tells a cautionary tale about a boy who could not resist a few biscuits to ease the hunger pangs before receiving the pure white host, the Son of God himself, on his tongue. As the boy opened his mouth to take

6

in the host, the priest saw that God had put a black stain over his tongue and realised the boy was not worthy to receive communion. Father Michael always took trouble to stress the shame of it. The priest sent the boy straight out of the church, declaring him to be in a state of Mortal sin. We all assumed the boy had burned for all eternity, somewhere along the road to Carlow.

In fear of sins, Mortal and Venial, sins of commission and sins of omission, sins of enjoyment and sins committed out of sheer boredom, in fact in fear of practically everything that is not downright unpleasant or actually painful, on the basis that if it is not unpleasant or painful it probably is a sin, we take our rumbling stomachs to church.

No-one complains. We live in a rigid and ordered world and know no other. My brother, Declan, and I, are altar servers. During the sermon my gaze strays over the congregation. Mary McDonagh is at the front of the side aisle. Her mother-of-pearl rosary beads glitter as they dangle from her plump, brown fingers. My one ambition in life is to tumble with her in her father's hay loft. I would gladly risk hell's fires for two hours getting to know her up there.

Father Michael glowers at his wayward flock. His neck bulges frighteningly as he restrains an almost overwhelming fury about something. We know not what. He exhorts us to avoid the occasions of sin. Impure thoughts are as bad as impure acts. Thinking about adultery and other sins of the flesh is as bad as performing the acts themselves. He pauses long and heavy to allow everyone to think seriously about adultery.

The altar boy beside me is Declan. He swings the thurible slowly and rhythmically throughout the silence. Ghostly white clouds swirl across the sanctuary and down the aisles. Emaciated flies bang themselves senseless against stained glass Saint Patrick standing in bare feet on the writhing snakes. Mary McDonagh's naked ankles, knees and lower thighs are enveloped by groping fingers of incense. Her curls give out a golden fire in the dustgleaming sunlight, but her eyes are hidden in prayerful shadow. She is untouchable under her gilded halo, wrapped in an aura of saintliness. Light and deep shade accentuate the proudness of her cheekbones and her perfectly

7

proportioned body, my Greek goddess, Mary McDonagh, The Holy Virgin of Bagenalstown.

"If thine eye offends, pluck it out," Father Michael bellows like a bull in pain, then changes to a threatening whisper, "Avoid even the smallest of wrongdoings lest they lead to greater ones and the inevitable loss of your immortal soul."

I feast my eyes on my ethereal vision, the epitome of innocent spirituality, moved deeply by her sensuous unavailability. I have seen her striding lithely through the long wet grass at her father's farm. I have watched her stroking the silken snouts of the horses there. I have marvelled as she controlled the huge beasts, riding bare-back and wild straight over thorny hedges and across the endless, swaying corn fields.

"The pleasures of the flesh are as nothing compared with the sublime delight achieved by self denial and self control. Be not blinded, dear brethren, by the shallow pleasures with which Lucifer tempts you; they are as nothing compared to the glories which await you if you are true to Him. He who watches us, and watches over us, every second of every minute of every day. He who gave His life for us in the ultimate sacrifice, at The Crucifixion. If ever you are tempted. And which one of us is not tempted?" Father Michael pauses meaningfully, "Can anyone here stand up before us now and say he or she has never been tempted to fornicate?" His eye moves systematically around the church for a response. No-one moves a muscle, apart from Ma O'Keefe who, we all know, suffers badly with her nerves. "Remember this. He is close at hand. He is watching you. He knows what is going on in your head. All you have to do is call on Him. He is the one Friend who will never, ever, let you down. Just call on Him whenever you begin to falter." Father Michael is beginning to subside. His neck deflates, his passion spent. "Now, dearly beloved, let us remember those Holy Souls being cleansed of their sins in the scorching flames of purgatory, even now as I speak, who, without the help of our special prayers, will take even longer to reach their eternal reward in Heaven. Out of the depths I have cried to you, O Lord. Lord, hear my voice..."

Father Michael looks relaxed and solemn. I am still in ecstacy. The summer's heat, the incense, my tweed suit overlaid with

8

thick, black cassock and lacy white surplice, lack of food and drink; all combine. My knees turn to water. At Father Michael's exhortation to pray, Mary lifts her head as if directing prayerful petitions heavenward, but her eyes stare directly at me. They pour their supernatural beauty into mine. Suddenly there is fire in my belly. My skin burns. I feel so weak and yet my body has developed a will of its own and is secretly preparing for the dance of love, despite the weight of my overgarments. I am convinced the whole congregation can see a tell-tale bulge at the front of my surplice. I curse Father Michael under my breath for insisting that the older altar boys stand up during the sermon because of the shortage of benches. I concentrate on reciting mathematical tables, but to no avail.

Mary alters her posture ever so slightly. She slides her hips forward slowly and deliberately, presumably to ease the pain from sitting still on the rock hard bench. Dancing black dots obscure my vision. Bombarded by a barrage of flashing lights, I feel only relief as I slide weightlessly to the highly polished, wood-block floor.

"It's a nice morning for it, Pop."

"Whaa... Whaaa... Ah, you're a great woman, Noreen. I live for a cuppa char in the mornings. Put it here where I can reach it, would yous?"

"It's over there on the table, by the window."

"I'll take it in a minute, then..."

"The cemetery today, remember? You wanted to go."

"I did, so I did."

"Cecil and Sean will take you up in the car."

"Ah, it's a great morning for it, Noreen. I'll be up and dressed in two shakes of a lamb's tail, tell Cecil, and thanks for the tea."

I select my black, patent leather shoes, grey flannels, cream sports coat and straw hat. It all takes time. These blessed longjohns take an age to get on and I always nick myself shaving when I rush. I must look my best for Mammy though.

"Ready, Pop? Cecil is waiting."

"I'll not be long, Noreen, once I've the longjohns on."

There is a discontented hubbub downstairs. Eventually, I descend the stairs very deliberately, not to be annoying but because my gait is very weak. The creaking stairs, fourth and third from the bottom, seem to mock me with the same, long drawn out groan every time I use them. The sound of my parchment dry hand inching along the handrail with the same bony swish even gets on my own nerves. It is so cautious. Yet I would probably get giddy and tumble if I rushed.

There are three flies circling the pink glass lampshade in the hallway. One lands on my shoulder as I pass beneath but I cannot brush it away. I have my walking stick in one hand and need to support myself on the hall table with the other. The fly now explores the pieces of tissue which staunch the blood flow at strategic points around my chin.

Outside I can see Cecil sitting at the roadside in the Ford Anglia. The engine is running. He is polishing the inside of the windscreen with a yellow duster. Now he is polishing his glasses with a large white handkerchief. A Saint Christopher medal adorns the dashboard. He begins to polish that with the white handkerchief. He is a smart fellow. Has a good education behind him and a steady job in the Civil Service. He sports a fine, closely-cropped but bristly, moustache.

"Can I help you, Grandad?" Suddenly a young voice pipes up behind me. I take hold of Sean's arm. He is a big man of seven. Down the garden steps he guides me. First the white marble one, then two large uneven ones, a quick tussle with the garden gate, then the last tiny step which often catches me out as I raise my hat civilly to a passer-by. Today I have Sean with me. He may be young but he has sturdy little legs and strong arms.

The Ford Anglia's paintwork is now gleaming in the sunlight. It is grey. I manage to get in without trapping my fingers in the door. It did happen once. Cecil thought I was in and slammed the door. It just caught the tips of three fingers on the left hand.

Driving along Cowbridge Road I try to help us forget we are going to the cemetery. I do not want to make life gloomy for little Sean.

"Had a good week at the office, Cecil?"

Cecil studies his rear view mirror intently. He is a very careful driver. You would trust him with your life. He polishes the rear view mirror with the yellow duster and frowns.

"Mmmm..."

You would have a terrible job to break Cecil's concentration when he is driving.

Cecil has always been quiet. Even as a child.

"It's a nice day for a drive out, Cecil, don't you think?"

"Yee..s."

Cecil is satisfied with the rear view mirror now and tosses the duster into the glove compartment.

We pass through Ely, by several pubs with thirst-provoking names like 'The Dusty Forge'. A little nip of Jameson's would not come amiss right now – just to soothe the throat. We leave the car outside the enormous cast iron gates and towering railings. I always wonder if they are designed to keep the buried people in or the live people out. Why do they have to separate us from each other? Cecil holds back respectfully. He always leaves me to find Mammy's grave on my own.

11

I suddenly feel ashamed to be wearing a straw hat. It seems too frivolous, disrespectful even. I take it off and hold it in front of me, against my chest. They say men cannot cry properly, but I try to. The whole scene shimmers gloriously through my wet-prism eyes. Handkerchief. I drop my hat. Little Sean retrieves it for me. There is the stone. Florence Connolly. Mammy is there. I do wish I could really let go. I sob and make a snuffling noise like a young boy with a runny nose. What sort of man calls his wife 'Mammy'? I do not care now. She is what matters. I picture her, before we moved to Cardiff to live with Cecil and Noreen. She pauses in the dining room of our house at Burnham-on-Sea. Felt like living back in 'the old country' when we lived in Somerset. She has just lifted the little muslin cloth off the jug. The jug which contains the cream skimmed off from the surface of the scalded milk. The cloth has tiny, blue, glass beads around its edge, which Mammy painstakingly stitched there, despite the trembling of her hands from the Parkinson's Disease which afflicted her for years. She wears a fawn, crocheted shawl around her shoulders. Her hair, slightly thinning and very fine, is pulled back in a bun.

"Come in, Pop," she chides, "Come and eat your breakfast. You'd be out in that garden all day if I didn't bully you." How ridiculous, a woman calling her husband 'Pop'. What were we like?

"Coming, Mammy. I'm coming." She stands there, slightly stooping, a gentle smile in the corners of her mouth. She is beautiful.

On our way home we take Sean to the swings in Llandaff Fields. Cecil shields his eyes from the sun and stares towards the village, "Now that, son," he announces to Sean, "That is the spire of Llandaff Cathedral. That used to be a Catholic Church before Henry the Eighth gave it to the Protestants." Sean's youthful exuberance causes him to fall off the witch's hat and he grazes his knee.

"I want to go home," he blubs, sitting beside me on the park bench.

"I think that other building, to the left of the Cathedral, may be the old Bishop's Palace. Of course, it's a ruin now..." Cecil has a great feeling for the history. Has shelves full of books in his room at home.

Sean's face is upturned to mine, "Did you go on the witch's hat, when you were a boy, grandad?"

"We'd no swings, Sean, just the countryside to play in, when I was growing up in Ireland," I look deep into his innocent eyes, "Enjoy your childhood years, lad. They are the happiest of your life." What I do not say is that they were my happiest years. I still had a land, a place to be, a people. I had not lost them then and I could simply enjoy the warm blood coursing through my veins, from heart to fingertip.

I feel my heart pumping again with life, not fear. I run like spindrift down to the river, instead of to the old school building in Bagenalstown. We always head for the deepest part of the river, my brothers and I. Once out of sight, we strip off, trudge down the dusty riverbank. From the sandy strand by the bridge, we swim like killer whales, monarchs of every shoal and current we swim through. We slice deep down through crystal waters to pick up stones from the river bed. It takes your breath away, bolts it tightly inside your lungs. It sets your teeth chattering. I can still feel the sun's warmth wrapped like a blanket around my body after swimming. I remember the fresh meadow grass and the openness of the sky. Lying on my back, infinity begins to mean something. I do not yet understand that all things are finite.

Swimming in the river's midstream race terrifies me because I know I am destined to live forever. It often causes me to strike out in panic for the river's bank. What if I inhale a mouthful by mistake? What if I get stomach cramps? Yet my fear is pleasure. I know I am safe. It is idle fun to imagine what it must feel like to drown. The moment you change from threshing about to floating like a rag doll. How does that feel? What will they all say if I float downstream past the schoolyard at breaktime? "Aw, God, there goes poor old Connolly. He was a gas of a feller, wasn't he, lads?"

"Sure he was, but he couldn't swim to save his life..."

There would be the funeral. The biggest ever held in Bagenalstown. Such a tragedy – going so young. His whole life before him. Father Michael would remind them all what a pious lad I was, an example to them all, a credit to my parents, a good altar boy and my soul probably free from all stain of sin with any luck, when he took my age into consideration. Mary McDonagh would be at the front of the procession, inconsolable, crying, "Oh, if only he had lived. We were to be married, you see. Or at least we were going to give things a good go up in my father's hay loft. May Eternal Light shine on him... such a sweet boy."

I do not drown. I grasp copious reeds to haul myself onto the river's bank. Mud oozes between my toes. My limbs are supple. My muscles feel fresh and strong as I wrestle on the bank with my brother, Declan.

I had a place then and my brothers did too. They were fine, handsome lads, John, Mick, Declan... and the rest of them. Their teeth were gleaming white. Like film stars' teeth, you could say. No grand farm for us to inherit. A small, rented house. Fine when we were children. There was not room for us as adults, not room for us to grow in Ireland. To America some went. Dominic went to be a priest in Nigeria. Did very well for himself. Became the Cardinal's assistant out there. Others did building work in England and drifted between there and home, not knowing where to settle. I joined the Army. The British Army. It was when everyone in Ireland was talking about 'Home Rule'. A few years after I joined up there was the Easter Rebellion. Later on the nationalists managed to set up an independent Irish government. That was why I never went back. I was no longer the man from Bagenalstown who liked to swim in the River Barrow. I heard bits of news, but I never met any of the family again, after I left. In the eyes of the folks back home, I was a British Tommy.

The British Army gave me a training which set me in good stead. In the signal corps I served. I clipped my speech. Used to try to talk like an Englishman at that time.

You were all reduced to the same level in the Army, whether you spoke like an aristocrat or an Irishman. The old joke they told was about the new recruit called Montague.

"Stand to attention, Montaig," says the Sergeant Major.

"The name is Mont-a-gue, Sir, if you don't mind," says the new recruit.

14

"Well, if that's what you want, Mont-a-gue, you can get started on four hours fat-i-gues for your trouble," says the Sergeant Major.

"We're off to France," one day the Company Sergeant Major announces. I see a lot of the insides of trenches and not a lot of France. The distance of a bus stop away we can see Fritz in his trenches. Shells whistle overhead. There is screaming. Incessant explosions. It gets on my nerves. My hand begins to shake so much, I am unable to send the messages. Aw, God, I send them alright. I would be shot otherwise for disobeying an order. It is just that the messages become indecipherable at the other end. At H.Q. they think I have been given the gift of tongues. In fact I am thinking I am in Hades and the world has come to an end. I am glad to get away from there alright. It takes me years to feel confident again. I do not want to go back to the old village in Ireland in case someone takes it into their head to shoot at me over there as well.

After the war I am stationed all over the country, Bulford Camp on Salisbury Plain, Carshalton in Surrey, and a dozen others I can picture but whose names I forget. Luckily I get a job in the Post Office on discharge.

The Post Office in Market Drayton is small but I remember it well because there I met Mammy.

Over the years we move from village to village. I find it hard to settle. When the baby arrives, we decide an English name would be nice. Cecil grew up a real little gentleman.

"Thank you, Cecil, for driving me to the cemetery."

"Half past ten," Cecil consults his watch.

"You've got a lot on. For the Church, is it?"

"Civil Service Catholic Guild. Typing."

"Ah, that's great work. Great work. I'll be up in my room then. See yous at lunch."

"How can I tell that these are the happiest days of my life, Grandad?" Sean is still rubbing his grazed knee.

Back in my room I switch on both bars of my electric fire. The sun is still shining outside. It is difficult to keep warm these days. I change into my slippers, zip them up as far as they will

15

go, press my hands as close to the fire as I can stand. The soft wool of the hearthrug under my feet is comforting. The old clock with the brass plaque ticks as steadily as when it was presented to me on my retirement. The strolling minstrels in porcelain strum their mandolins in time with its beat. Mammy's brother gave us those. All my things bring back memories. The older I get, the older my memories seem to be. For some reason it is Mary McDonagh's face which drifts before me as often as not these days. I am getting warmer. I must admit I welcome her intrusion, whether it be into my dreams or into my thoughts, because everything I recall about that time seems so vivid to me now. I get to know her properly at Declan's fifteenth birthday party. We talk a lot but it is the physical things which stay with me most. She has on a simple, red dress which exposes her arms. The material is a kind of hessian. Not unlike the material of the sofa I am sitting on. She pulls me by the hand into the kitchen, after we have discussed the weather for about half an hour, just as the others are getting going with some Irish reels. I remember how she feels through that dress. I remember how she pushes herself against me as we kiss. Heady stuff for a young lad prone to fainting fits on the altar. Eating strawberries and cream always reminds me of those first kisses. It gets me down now of course, picking the strawberry seeds out of my teeth.

"I've seen you looking at me."

"You have?"

"Did you like what you saw?"

"Y' I did that."

"Put your hand there, Connolly. Is that all right for you?"

She is a young woman of great character. I develop the greatest respect for her directness. It is wonderful. Possibilities, fearful questions, career around my head. Mary likes me for sure. Would I dare, if she really wanted me, to show her how hotly I care for her? Would I dare? There is a clock in a mahogany case on the kitchen wall. Mary's breath caresses my cheek as softly as a butterfly's wings. Short, tense breaths, faster than the ticking of the clock. The others keep passing the kitchen door. They are snorting with laughter. I picture them winking at each other, puffing on their Sweet Afton cigarettes, trying not to inhale. Then sounds of panic. I hear Declan whisper, "Empty those ashtrays, quick!" The adults are back from the pub. It is time for Mary to return home with her father.

I move over to the window. There is a small private school across the road. A high wall runs around it, glass fragments cemented into the top. Marlborough House School. After the Duke of Marlborough, hero of victories at Blenheim and Malplaquet, I have always assumed. Our address is 206, Marlborough Hill. I live in a desirable area now alright. We celebrate the noble history of the British Army every time we mention where we live. I do believe Cecil chose the house because of its obvious associations. No children in the school today. Saturday. Only perfectly trimmed lawns in the school grounds. Parallel stripes, different shades of green, neatly formed ranks of troops, Irish Guards on parade.

During the week, I spend a lot of time watching the children. Screaming, shouting, laughing, in their emerald, serge uniforms. The bell tolls. Sudden, uncanny silence. Lessons. Then mayhem unleashed again at breaktime. I dislike the silence over there at weekends. The children's liveliness takes my mind off painful thoughts. When there is nothing to watch I rub the shiny skin on my scalp with the flat of my palm, conjure up foolish thoughts. Sometimes I slip back into thinking of myself as lonely. Self-pity. Such nonsense.

Over and beyond the cedar trees in the school, I can just see the roof of the Rhymney Brewery. The red neon sign there blazes out its presence every night. Noreen has been discouraging me from taking any alcohol recently. She says she read an article which said alcohol aggravates the lining of the stomach. At about the same distance, Fairwater rises and, to its left, Ely, where Mammy lies at rest. I can say 'hello' to her whenever I want, in the sky see her eyes as blue as the ocean.

Stretching forward, I look down the hill, past the Turog bakery, to the small Post Office run by Angus from Aberdeen. In the far distance, Leckwith Hill and its bluebell woods run east to the coast at Penarth.

Angus knows I am an old Postmaster. He is kind to me. Each

Thursday when I collect my pension, he looks me straight in the eye. He can tell how I am immediately. If he thinks I need cheering up he takes off his thick, tortoise-shell glasses and says, "Let's have a little chat today, Mr Connolly." He decided I needed sorting out a couple of days ago.

"The top of the morning to you, Angus..."

"There's a quiver in your voice today, my lad. You need to get out and about more."

"No, really. I'm fine. Musn't complain..."

"The Oasis Club..."

"The whaa'..."

"Opens lunchtime on Thursdays."

"Whe'...?"

"Just off Cowbridge Road. D'y ken Lion Road?"

"I think I do..."

"It'll cheer you up no end."

"No, really. I'm fine. Musn't..."

"Hell of a show. You'll love it."

"Well. I could..."

"Beginning of Lion Road. On the left. Yellow door."

"...just pop in."

Outside in the sunshine I pat my wallet, undecided. Angus is right. I have not been on an outing for a long while. Mammy and I used to go to Burnham-on-Sea Bowling Club nearly every day. Noreen and Cecil are wonderful company but they lead such busy lives. I might make some new friends at a club. I am feeling stronger than I have done for some time. It is decided.

When I get back, Noreen is polishing the silver with Duraglit, ready for a forthcoming dinner party. I change into my bottle-green trilby and navy-blue suit. I select a polished ebony walking stick, having replaced the rubber tip with a fresh, unused one.

"I'll be taking my lunch out today, Noreen."

"Righto, Pop."

"See yous later then."

"You've the fresh handkerchief with you?"

"I have that."

"The clean socks?"

"I do."

"The ones I put out for you first thing this morning?"

"Yis, yis, I do. I do... and I have on the elasticated stockings for the veins."

"I was going to ask about them."

"Oh..."

"They're not down around your ankles, I hope?"

"They are where they should be..."

"Good."

"Thank you, Noreen."

"Tea at six. Don't be late."

I stroll up Victoria Avenue, past Mrs O'Brien's house. Paddy is stretched out on the front door step enjoying the sunshine. He gets up unsteadily. Probably exhausted from overmuch procreation. He sidles up to me and licks my hand. I only wish Mrs O'Brien would do the same. She was widowed many years ago. Grew up in Sligo. Still a very fine woman. Her bronze curls glitter yet, even more brightly than Paddy's golden retriever coat.

I take a breather, hoping she might come out. She is nowhere to be seen. I wipe Paddy's saliva off my hands with my fresh handkerchief. The one Noreen put out for me first thing this morning. I love to converse with Mrs O'Brien. It is an education. She knows a great deal about the breeding of dogs. Of late we have been discussing the complexities of their mating behaviour in some depth. We have a favourite bench in Clarence Park. Beside a beautiful lily pond filled with gold-fish. In the centre is a plinth. On it a bronze statue of a naked youth. He is on tiptoe. Arms uplifted. He seems to be embracing creation with total naturalness, communing with a life force we can only glimpse. He reaches upward, his right arm a little higher than his left. He stretches, taut, graceful. Fountains spring high into the air around him. He is cascaded with water droplets which become rivulets coursing over and around every contour of his body. Mrs O'Brien tends to look in his direction during lulls in our conversation. Fondles the soft, furry skin around Paddy's ears. Paddy's eyes glaze over. She stroked my bottle-green trilby, where it lay on the bench between us, by mistake one day. I think she feels sympathy for me. Having lost Mammy. Brings back thoughts of her own loss.

The perfume from the flower beds, as I pass the statue in midday heat, revives happy memories of recent meetings with Mrs O'Brien in the park. But I am tiring. Perspiration escapes from beneath my hat's leather lining. I dab my forehead with my handkerchief. The aroma of flowers mingles strangely with the smell of dried dog saliva.

I whistle along Daisy Road. The art of happiness is to live as if we are going to live forever. I got that from a matchbox. England's Glory, I think. The starlings join in. I have not walked so far since Mammy's funeral procession, over six months ago. Outside The Oasis Club my legs feel as if they have just carried me through a heavy bog, after rain. Leaning gratefully on my stick, I tap on the yellow door. A flap opens at eye level. After a few moments, a man whispers from the void within. He has a local accent.

"You rang, like?"

I find myself whispering back, despite the noise of motor cars in the background.

"Can I enter?"

"Member?"

"Yes... Sorry, no. I'm not... but I..."

"Members only, grandad. Sorry, like."

"Wait, young man, wait. Your establishment, er... highly recommended, er... very close friend of mine, er..."

"Who's that, then?"

"Angus. From the Post Office on Marlborough Hill."

"Oh, 'im. E's 'armless enuf."

"I certainly find him so. He said there's a hell of a good show on here... said I would love it."

"No kiddin'."

"On my word of honour."

"A'rite... tempary member... come in and sign the book... just for today, mind."

I feel my way forward in total darkness. Slowly my eyes adapt. A yellow orb imbues the scene with the faintest ochre glow. Ten burnished gold pillars surround the floorspace. Through a window alcove three pyramids, palm trees, and donkeys, no, camels. A lake – that must be the oasis. Miles of

desert stretch to a horizon which melts into a white-hot sky. I
have been transported surely to an ancient Egyptian palace.
Organ music adds to the magical atmosphere. I cannot place the
tune. Reminds me of something on Noreen and Cecil's T.V.
They invite me to watch it with them oftentimes in the evenings.
I think it is one of them new-fangled advertisement tunes. For
Fry's Turkish Delight. That is the one. Very nice it is too.

Tables and chairs are neatly arranged. At one table a man sits
smoking, staring at the yellow orb.

The heat is like that in the desert itself. What with the un-
accustomed exercise, I have a terrible drouth on me. Behind the
pillars, a sign bearing simple, illuminated hieroglyphics. My
spectacles are misted over. I can make out a snake shape, like
an 'S'. Then a pyramid shape. It could be an 'A'. 'S.A.' – the
Lord be praised, it is a beer pump. I step forward, terrified I
might tread on an asp at any moment, or a half-clothed beggar
lurking in the shadows to prey on unwary travellers.

"A pint, please."

"S.A. or bitter?"

"What is the S.A.?"

"Tha's the Special Ale... but we calls it Skull Attack... it's the
strong 'un."

"Go on, I'll take a pint of the S.A."

It slides down like a pint of oysters. And the next one does.
The fellow behind the bar makes you feel welcome.

"A grand place, this."

"Yer furst time 'ear, isit?"

"'Tis so... but I'll be coming again."

"Show'll be startin' now, in a minit. Luverly singer that Tony
Boyle."

I move across to the tables and chairs.

"Would you mind if I joined you, sir?"

The man staring at the yellow orb does not seem to hear me
but he has such a lovely serene smile on his face I sit down at
the same table. A man in a dinner jacket steps onto a rostrum
at the front.

"Arr'rite then... Welcum to lunchtime a' Cairdiff's very own
O.. A.. SIS CLU..B. We gotta grrr'ate show line dup f'you.
Mike on the argan, furst. Then the cabarray. So, 'opes you

enjoys it, like. An'now givva warm welcum to Mike – on the biggust argan in town."

There are only the two of us in the audience. People do not get their pay until Friday, I suppose. My table companion and I begin to get to know each other while Mike goes through his repertoire.

"They do a fine pint in here, don't you think?"

"Cool..."

"Spot on. Yes. Just what yis need on a scorcher like today... and the organ player there. He has a fine technique – very contemporary. That Ben Hur music is real hot stuff, isn't it?"

"Ben Hur... yeah, man... cool..."

"Yes, indeed. Quite so. Would you care for a fresh pint?"

My friend pushes his glass across without taking his gaze off the yellow orb. He still has the cheeky grin on his face.

Mike has finished on the organ. The man in the dinner jacket announces, "A'now it's time for Tony Boyle from the Shamrock Ayul. Thank..u. A big 'and please f'T...ONY."

Tony is a tenor. He sings with all his heart.

"WHEN FIRST I SAW THE LOVE LIGHT IN YOUR EYE

I DREAMED THE WORLD HELD NOUGHT BUT JOY FOR ME

AND EVEN THOUGH WE DRIFTED FAR APART

I NEVER DREAM BUT WHAT I DREAM OF THEE"

This is lovely. He has a beautiful voice.

"I LOVE YOU AS I'VE NEVER LOVED BEFORE

SINCE FIRST I MET YOU ON THE VILLAGE GREEN

COME TO ME, ERE MY DREAM OF LOVE IS O'ER

I LOVE YOU AS I LOVED YOU

WHEN YOU WERE SWEET

WHEN YOU WERE SWEET SIXTEEN"

This is the life. What a singer. I hum along with him. I am full of tenderness. Grateful to have lived and loved. I want all I have known and who have reached out to me to be part of a vast, caring, loving family. No arguments. No jealousies. Just helping each other, holding each other, warm in each other's arms. I imagine us together, overcoming pain, fear and human frailty. I pat my new friend on the back, show him a thumbs up.

23

I am so moved. He sways, nearly falls off his chair, stabilises. The doorman, the barman, the man in the dinner jacket and I create a tumultuous applause. Tony Boyle reaches his last number.

"I WILL TAKE YOU HOME AGAIN, KATHLEEN
ACROSS THE OCEAN WIDE AND WILD
TO WHERE YOUR HEART HAS EVER BEEN
SINCE FIRST YOU WERE MY BLUSHING BRIDE

THE ROSES ALL HAVE LEFT YOUR CHEEKS
I'VE WATCHED THEM FADE AWAY AND DIE
YOUR VOICE IS SAD WHEN ERE YOU SPEAK
AND TEARS BEDIM MY LOVING EYE"

I picture Mammy on her death bed. All white sheets and hollow cheeks.

"I WILL TAKE YOU BACK, KATHLEEN
TO WHERE YOUR HEART WILL FEEL NO PAIN
AND WHEN THE FIELDS ARE FRESH AND GREEN
I WILL TAKE YOU TO YOUR HOME, KATHLEEN"

The sadness in Tony's voice is almost too much to bear. It touches me deep inside. My glasses steam up again. Not because of the heat this time.

The man in the dinner jacket is back. "'Ank you, TO....NY BOYLE. Absulootly friggin' maavelus, tha'wuz..."

It is time to go. It has been an interesting outing, but I am drained. It has been a visit I would not have missed but it must now be close to tea-time.

"A'now the e-qully maavelus, eggsotic and bee-ootiful TAN-Y-A..."

The cabaret has more than one act. My table companion is going? No.

"My round, mate. Pint of Skull Attack, O.K.?"

"Surely. Very kind of you. That'll be... cool." It might be a mistake to refuse. I have no wish to upset the man.

Tanya is swathed in yards of purple material edged with gold foil. A gauze veil covers her face. Mike is back on the organ playing soothing, rhythmic music. I wonder whether they are bringing in a religious twist to end the cabaret. The Egyptian equivalent of God Save The Queen at the end of The Proms. Tanya sways gently in time with the music, as if in a trance. From somewhere behind the rostrum they are burning something. Sweet-smelling smoke is drifting everywhere. It gets in your throat. I tackle my pint. Slowly, slowly, Tanya is uncovering a python. Coiled tightly around her chest, her waist and one of her legs. She lets fall her robes and veil to the floor. Shoves them off the rostrum with a deft flick of her free foot. She wears a pink, silken swimsuit affair, black stockings, high heels. She is a stunner alright. Now she is down on the floor doing some kind of gymnastics with the python. She survives that and approaches our table. Her black hair is as smooth as oil. "Go on. Stroke it, love. It won't bite you." She insists we stroke it. My table mate seems to be coming around. I get the impression he has been before. "It's cool. They crushes you if they get angry."

The music is building to a crescendo. Tanya kisses the python on its nose. Disentangles herself from its coils. Leaves it writhing on one side of the rostrum. I watch it carefully. There is nothing between it and me. The yellow orb is dipping up and down, circling the area above the rostrum. Part of the act, an optical illusion, the Skull Attack? Holy Mother of God, Tanya is taking the swimsuit and stockings off. The music has changed tempo. It is the Turkish Delight again. Does she know what she is about at all? All she has on her is a triangular scrap of maroon velvet, held in place with string. Oh, Glory... she has tassels swinging from her nipples. That must be so painful. How on earth are they attached? I cannot look. Tony is raising the tempo yet again. I hide my face in my pint glass. Through the frothy semi circle at the bottom of the glass, I cannot help taking in Tanya jumping hard up and down to the music. The tassels are twirling at a fierce speed, like aeroplane propellors. Next to me my friend's eyes are spinning in his head. This is not good. She should not have to do this. She could surely damage herself for life. Ruin her marriage prospects. I must do something. I rise. Head for the rostrum. I try to slip off my jacket as I go. Tanya is still jumping, jumping, like a mad thing. I crash into tables and chairs in my haste. The floor of the rostrum is creaking and bending to breaking point. The python is levitating briefly then thumping back down uncontrollably. It looks distressed. I have to risk it.

"Here, my dear. Stop. Take my coat... go on... Do, please."

Mike stops playing the music. Tanya can hear me properly now.

"Tanya... you could hurt yisself... hurt yisself badly doing that. Come home with me... Noreen'll give yis a nice cuppa..."

"Get stuffed, you... ASSHOLE."

Tanya retreats to the back of the rostrum, glaring. The python decides I was responsible for making it bounce so unpleasantly. It glides towards me. Mike starts up the music again. The whispering doorman takes me firmly by the arm. Puts his mouth close to my ear. "Time to go 'ome, chummy. Now."

"Yis, yis. I'm sorry." I whisper into his ear, "Sorry for any inconvenience... don't know what I was thinking of at all..."

The tassels are back in normal service once again. I decide not to wave goodbye.

"I'll be on my way, then."

The doorman leans over me. "You're too pissed, grandad. We'll phone your family for you."

Noreen will have finished polishing the silver. Will probably have been starching the damask table cloth and serviettes in good time for the dinner party. Will have laid up for tea already, to give her a chance to put her feet up for five minutes. I am caught between a rock and a hard place.

"Mrs Connolly? Oasis Club 'ere. Grandad's not well. We're sendin' 'im 'ome in a taxi, arright?"

The doorman puts the receiver down as if it has bitten him. "She says, 'Over her dead body'. If you waits outside someone called Cecil will come and collect you."

Outside, I blink and stagger in the afternoon sunlight. Move away from the yellow door. Stand outside Pope's, the Cowbridge Road photographic shop. Cecil will prefer that. He is a keen photographer. He may not know The Oasis Club. I stand at attention. Military training and discipline have succoured me so often in my life. I feel a little acidity at the back of my throat. Ignore it. Breathe deeply. In. Out. In. Out. Hold

26

it in. Concerted effort. No. There it goes. On the word 'Out'. Into the gutter. Half of it ends up in my trouser turn-ups. 'Stomach Attack' not 'Skull Attack', they should call that beer. A trolley bus just misses me. Jesus, Mary and Joseph – assist me in my last agony.

At least I have not been sick on the pavement. The last thing these good people want, out doing their afternoon shopping, is to be confronted with an obstruction of that sort. I see Cecil. Way down the road, outside Peacocks. I weave towards him between the pushchairs and the shopping baskets. Something is on my mind. I cannot bring it into focus. Membership. The club membership. I forgot to get a form. Cecil has spotted me. Best to leave it.

"Thanks a million, Cecil. For coming down. A funny turn I had. Came over me all of a sudden."

Cecil has noticed my trouser turn-ups. He gets the yellow duster from the glove compartment. Carefully places it under my feet. Kind of him not to mention why.

"I hope this is not putting you out too much, Cecil?"

Cecil is his usual patient self. Breathing hard through his nose is his way of showing me he understands.

"Take those trousers off, straightaway." Noreen is waiting in the hallway. I feel like a small child as I struggle out of them. Cecil has to help me as I sit on the hallway chair that is only there for decoration.

"Please, please. Don't trouble yourself on my account, Noreen. I'm such a sucker for the biliousness though, am't I?"

I pull myself up the stairs. Dare not let go of the banister.

Noreen calls after my disappearing shirt tails and longjohns, "I've heard things about that place, Pop... Not nice things either..."

I visualise the plucky way Tanya handled that python. Close up, her legs were a mottled purple colour. Thin. A spirited creature, begob.

"No, it's not nice there, Noreen. It's a terrible dump." I think maybe I will not go again. Not until I am over Mammy's death. If ever that day dawns. Maybe then.

That evening a sense of elation consumes me, followed by a dead numbness. Angus will laugh at my adventure. "Mr Connolly, you're a real old soldier." His head will go back. His mouth open wide with silent mirth. "You're like Bruce and the spider. You neverrr gi'up." The Post Office stamp in his right hand, he will pummel his ink pad and piled forms faster than a pneumatic drill. "This is it, not a dress rehearsal. Life doesn't give second chances, does it, Mr Connolly? Oh, no." A bit of a philosopher is Angus. The numbness is a more vague feeling. A sense of unease, restlessness. I pick up an old photograph. The staff and pupils of the Christian Brothers Boys School at Recknaw Abbey, where the bright boys went. Where I went when I was eleven.

"You're the cream of the county, you lads." ('Clotted, clotted,' the required response.) Brother Benignus is the Head. Wiry hair, like an unravelling scouring pad. Broken teeth, at all angles. No eyelashes. Fingers and thumbs, tawny-brown from smoking. Belly and grey vest bursting through the front of a threadbare soutane. Soft, black leather shoes. Moves around like a panther. Kind and affectionate. Sits the new boys on his knee. How they giggle when he gets his heavy, leather strap out. Has blonde-haired favourites. Tickles them. Explodes with rage for no reason. Laughs uproariously whenever a boy looks perplexed or confused. Metes out discipline, when necessary, sternly.

Discipline is particularly strict at morning assembly. We congregate in lines. Each class forms up in pairs about seventeen deep. Brother Benignus makes his announcements and then, to start the day, we recite five decades of The Rosary.

In the first year, my friend, O'Reilly, and I, discover we can hold a civilised conversation during The Rosary if we position ourselves at the very back. The results of hurling matches and where the best horse chestnuts are to be had – so long as we speak during the prayers and not during the pauses – are exchanged this way throughout most of two terms.

Towards the end of the second term, we are ducking down comparing the sizes of our cocks one morning. We had both noticed a growth spurt and were worried we might not be normal.

"B'jaysus, O'Reilly. You've got a monster! Do yis have to strap it to your leg yet?"

"Yer an eejit, Connolly. So, how about you? Are you a mouse or a man? Come on, out with it. Don't be shy..."

"I've nothing to be ashamed of, O'Reilly. At least I'm not tripping over mine... yet. Come on out, Peetee..."

O'Reilly is nearly rolling on the floor with laughter.

"Why do you call your cock, 'Peetee'?"

"It's always been called that... It's its name... I can't remember why."

"And where in God's name has the end of it gone, Connolly?" O'Reilly sounds frightened and concerned for me at one and the same time.

"Can it happen to anyone? Can it be repaired at all?"

O'Reilly is talking too loudly.

"Quiet, O'Reilly."

He begins to see the funny side of things again.

"Have you got leprosy or wha'?"

"Shut it, will yer."

"Did y'catch it in the front door?"

"Of course not."

"You weren't born like that, surely?"

"No."

"And you're sure it's not contagious?" He looks anxious again at the thought that it might be and tucks his own exhibit back into his pants.

Brother Benignus is leading the school into the second Sorrowful Mystery of The Rosary, The Scourging of Jesus.

"...And so let us be mindful, as we contemplate the sufferings experienced by Jesus for our sins, of the terrible wounds and humiliations He endured for our sakes; let us be mindful of the countless cruel slights and hurts which we inflict on others, those around us, those we love, in our daily lives. Every single one of us. Every day of our lives. And let us thank Our Lord

29

for taking all our sins and wrongdoings onto His own pure and faultless shoulders to free us from the tyranny of sin and to allow us to enter into everlasting happiness in His eternal kingdom... Our Father, who art in heaven..."

O'Reilly has settled down again. I want him to understand.

"I've been circumcised, is all."

"Ah, sure the size is not so bad, Connolly. It's the appearance that would worry me."

"It means I had the end cut off – when I was a little squealer."

"Yer poor sod," O'Reilly looks pale.

"But did ya know Jesus hisself was circumcised?" We both bow our heads as taught at the mention of His name.

"He was?"

"All Jewish babies had it done eight days after birth."

"Y'can't fool me, Connolly. Sure, Jesus was a Catholic."

"A Catholic and a Jew, O'Reilly... He was done just the same as me. But in His case He was officially given the name the Angel had given Him before His conception, at the same time."

"Would y'credit it? It figures though, mind you."

"It's what the Bible tells us, O'Reilly."

"I don't tink me own parents heard about that or they'd most like have had me done the same. I should have thought they would, so."

"Not a lot of people do know about it, y'see."

"So that's it, then. That's why y'had it done?"

"I'm not really sure, O'Reilly."

"Are y'not?"

"Well, y'see... me mother told me the Arab people have it done a lot, too."

"Catholics, Jews... and Arabs?"

"She said it was something to do with cleanliness. Stops the desert sand getting stuck under the foreskin, y'see. Saves hours and hours at the pump. A real godsend it is."

"Well, I never."

"Y'probably got half the strand at Bray under yours last summer, O'Reilly."

"Piss off, Connolly. I've more sense than that."

O'Reilly is laughing out loud again. I want to check something with him before we move off the subject.

"Does yours go hard sometimes, O'Reilly?"

"Sure it does."

"Mine went hard when I was on the Altar the other day..."

"Mine does that every morning... for hours on end... all the time."

SMACK. STARS EXPLODE BEFORE MY EYES. AGAIN THE BACK OF MY HEAD IS STRUCK AS IF BY A ROCK. As I fall, a black shape flits past me and chops O'Reilly twice to the kidneys. I catch my ankle in the leather strap of my satchel. Go sprawling. I lie on my back, too dazed and disorientated to move. My Peetee droops sheepishly between my fly buttons. I wonder how long Brother Benignus has been watching us.

"What filt' has been going on here?"

"Nothing, Brother... Only saying The Rosary."

Brother Benignus averts his gaze, "Put that thing away, Connolly, immediately."

"Yis... Sorry, Brother."

"How dare you? How dare you? Ye've been blathering while the other boys have been reciting their Rosary."

"Oh, no, Brother. We've been saying The Joyful Mysteries with the rest."

"I'll give y'Joyful Mysteries, Mr Connolly." Brother Benignus pulls me to my feet by my hair, O'Reilly's scalp is in his other hand. "Go and wait outside my office. The both of yous."

The other boys are twisting their necks around to see what is going on. The Rosary is losing its impetus. Brother Benignus roars at them, "Carry on... Don't stop, don't stop... I'll strap the first boy that is not praying... 'Holy Mary, Mother of God, pray for us sinners now, and at the hour of our death, Amen.'"

As we leave the hall, Brother Benignus is already back on stage, head bowed, eyes closed, hands joined across his paunch, leading them into the third Sorrowful Mystery, The Crowning Of Jesus With Thorns, .. "and forgive us our trespasses, as we forgive those who trespass against us..."

I loved that school. It was the most god-forsaken place imaginable. It got under your skin. You had a great education. They beat it into you, so you never lost it. I learned to love poetry, history, Latin – could recite pages and pages of

Lucretius from memory. It opened your mind. It got me in the habit of reading for life. Later in life I embraced the work of W.B. Yeats, his dreams of a world free from the usual sadnesses of life, his quest for unachievable beauty. Life at Recknaw Abbey was totally down to earth. There was clear-cut guidance about right and wrong, during religious retreats where silence was observed for days on end. Questions to the visiting priest were put via an anonymous question box. The theme one year was 'How To Behave'. We were assured that you must not touch your own body. Under any circumstances. Nor let anyone else touch it. Apart from a Doctor of the same sex. Where other people were concerned, you must leave them alone, too. Many unpleasant diseases would be passed on if this was ignored. Keep very still until you are married. The worst thing imaginable is to give a girl a child before she is married. Getting married too young creates terrible difficulties. Rely on prayer and Christian love and all will be well. It certainly gave you something to hang on to.

The intellectuals, like Michael Olenga, the art teacher, used to argue it would be better to mix boys and girls in the same school. We laughed our heads off at the very thought. It seemed so implausible. Brother Benignus put into words what was obvious to all right thinking people in the school... "Co-education would be a total disaster. There would be hampered freedoms for the boys and possible moral evils for both sexes, if ever, God forbid, it came to pass. Putting the two together would be an obvious denial of Original Sin and a confusion of the real relationship of the two sexes." We did not understand it but we knew Brother Benignus was right. He could sound very authoritative about some things. Michael Olenga never got promotion during my time at the school.

Outside Brother Benignus's office, O'Reilly and I wait as if for Judgement Day. "It'll be six on the arse and a letter to our parents," O'Reilly is sure. We hear loud slapping noises approaching from around the corner. Brother Benignus sweeps into view. He is slashing out at the corridor walls with his strap. Bits of plaster fly everywhere. "Connolly, O'Reilly, Connolly, O'Reilly..." he chants, ritually avenging our heinous deeds. "Face the wall, boys. Jackets up. Now, are y'ready for this...?"

"Yes, brother," we chime in unison, hoping our subservience will lessen his wrath.

"Right, then. The first thing. Y'll both stand at the front of class lines at assembly from now on. Is that clear?"

"Yes, brother," we shout, in a froth of anticipation, waiting for the first lashes to fall.

"Now. Get out of my sight and behave yourselves. I won't be so lenient another time."

A few days later I am at the church for Confession. It was somewhere to send us when we were all at home on Saturday mornings. I have sinned. I must make a good examination of my conscience. I sit wriggling by the wall, working out what to say, trying to find the right words. Every word Ma O'Keefe says comes clear through the Confessional Box door and distracts me. She thinks because she cannot see the priest she must shout. She is as innocent as the day she was born.

I feel bad. I know if I get it right God will forgive me. Father Michael told us when he was preparing us for our First Confession that if we got knocked down and killed by a carriage immediately after we came out of Confession we would go straight to Heaven. We would be in a Perfect State Of Grace. I hoped I would be flattened after Confession for quite a while after that. When any little thing goes wrong after the Confession, nothing feels quite right until just after the next Confession.

It is getting more and more difficult. Putting my wrongdoings into words. I showed O'Reilly my cock during assembly and told him about circumcision. What sort of a sin was it? Not a sin of pride anyway. A sin of not joining in school prayers? A sin of upsetting Brother Benignus? Did I offend against any of the Ten Commandments? Thou shalt not covet thy neighbour's foreskin? I think not. I caused O'Reilly to get into trouble? Sure, he was talking just as much as I was. Did I insult O'Reilly? Called his cock a monster. That showed a lack of charity, I suppose. I looked at O'Reilly's cock. There we have it. That was a sin. That is not allowed. Best keep it simple. I can call it an 'impure act'.

There was that evening with Mary at my brother's fifteenth

birthday party. We both got very excited. Then again there was what I was thinking that morning when I fainted on the altar. Three 'impure acts' already. No. Two 'impure acts', one 'impure thought'.

Ma O'Keefe is really scraping the kettle clean, "I THOUGHT IT WAS THURSDAY. SO I DID NOT GO, FATHER. I MISSED MASS THAT SUNDAY, ALTOGETHER. SO WHEN I WENT THERE ON THE WEDNESDAY AT ELEVEN O'CLOCK, THE CHURCH WAS CLOSED, ALL LOCKED UP. I COULD HAVE EATEN ME HAT ON THE SPOT. WILL THAT BE A MORTAL SIN, FATHER?" The priest murmurs in a low, reassuring tone. I just catch what he says.

"Not if the intention was absent, my daughter."

"THE WHAA', FATHER? WILL I GO TO HELL? WILL I... WILL I?"

I cannot think of any more sins to confess. I need at least one other or the priest will be sure to ask questions about what the impure acts and thoughts involved. I have it. I forgot to say my evening prayers twice. That is always a good one. It makes it sound as if most of the time you are practically perfect. Another. I disobeyed my parents once. They told me to polish my boots before school.

Ma O'Keefe has finished. Her lips already silently mouth the prayers she has been given for her Penance. Forgiveness. In an ecstacy of relief she stands rooted, half in and half out of the Box.

The door to the Confessional Box rests half open when the Box is empty. As you step forward, it swings fully open and then closes of its own accord. Afterwards, it opens as you rise from your knees and shuts as you leave. I always thought this was a supernatural phenomenon, linked somehow to the miracle that takes place within the Box, the wiping away of one person's sins by another, acting on behalf of God.

On this occasion, Ma O'Keefe's exaltation lasts too long. The door bashes into the backs of her heels with a thump. She jumps as if struck by a bolt from heaven, scurries anxiously to a bench to pray. I discovered when I was older that the priest controlled the door with a complicated cord and pulley mechanism.

I nip in as unobtrusively as possible. Wait until the door is fully closed behind me.

"Pray Father, a blessing, for I have sinned. It is four weeks since my last confession." Total silence. Perhaps the priest thought Ma O'Keefe was the last and has gone. I wait for a full minute. At last there is a quiet cough.

"Go on, my son. What are you waiting for?" The voice is Father Michael's.

I direct my voice towards the wire grille. A black curtain covers the other side. "Since my last confession, I have done impure acts on two occasions and had impure thoughts on one occasion. I have forgotten to say my evening prayers twice and disobeyed my parents once. That is all I can remember, Father."

Father Michael pauses, as if considering these sins. I just want him to give me absolution so I can get out of the Box.

"There is one important thing I want to say to you, before you leave this box. Don't let me forget."

"No, Father," 'What's this about?', I think to myself.

"Now, about this disobedience to your parents. What did that involve?"

"Not cleaning my boots when I was told to. On just one occasion, Father."

"Ah, I see... I see... Well now, you must always listen to your parents. After all they brought you into this world and have cared for you all your life. They are the most important people. Treat them like Jesus treated His parents. Even God had to obey his parents, y'see. You will remember that, won't y'?"

"I shall, Father." I begin my Act of Contrition, hoping to move things along. "I confess to Almighty God..."

"One minute, my son. About these impure acts. Were they carried out on your own or with others? Mmmmm?"

"There was someone there on both occasions, Father."

"Oh, dear... and what term would describe the sort of activity that was going on? Take your time now. No need to rush."

"I'm not really sure, Father."

"How can I put this now?... Would you call it, er... foreplay, or more, er..."

"Oh, just foreplay, Father."

"I see, right, right, good... And these impure thoughts now. What about those?"

"I had those all on my own, Father."

"I didn't really mean... er... there you are then, my son. Well, all I can say is do try to do your best, your very best, from now on. Will y'? And above all, don't forget those evening prayers before you go off to sleep. Remember those and you won't go far wrong."

"I'll not, Father."

"Now, thank God for a good Confession. Make a sincere Act of Contrition, say three Hail Marys for your Penance and pray for me." Suddenly Father Michael whips back the curtain and pushes his face up to the grille... "And while I think of it, pop over to the Jumble Sale in the Church Hall for me, Connolly. Tell yer mother there've been some clothes left at the priests' house for the Saint Vincent de Paul's stall. She'll be able to include them in the sale."

The door opens smartly. I have not even recited my Act of Contrition. The heads of the people waiting outside look up to see who is coming out of the Box. I feel as if I am walking naked down the aisle, all eyes fixed on me in judgmental gaze. I avoided the Confessional Box after that but I still think of Father Michael from time to time. Perhaps that is a kind of prayer.

When I need to unburden myself these days, I talk to Tonga, Noreen's cat. Noreen had her when the Queen of Tonga visited London for the Coronation of our own Queen Elizabeth. Noreen really took to the Queen of Tonga. Tonga hears me out with an indifferent stare, as if to say, "Do you really think your little worries and transgressions are of any significance, Connolly? This is really a waste of my time." When I have told her everything, she brushes herself against my legs. Her expression implies, "For your Penance, you will get me lots of juicy tit-bits and a saucer of fresh milk." By then, I am absolved of my sins, cured of any worries. A weight is lifted from my shoulders, but only after I have forced my aching joints to get Tonga's milk down in front of her without spilling a drop, and risked Noreen's ire stealing choice slivers of lamb from the pantry.

DING... DING... DING... The bell rings thrice. Sanctus, sanctus, sanctus, Dominus Deus Sabaoth; Pleni sunt coeli et terra gloria tua. Hosanna in excelsis... What am I doing on my knees? Old habits die hard. Noreen is ringing the bell downstairs to call me down for lunch. I am like a man diving for the duck-boards every time a shell whistles overhead. I struggle to my feet. We shall taste the richness of the earth for lunch. Holy, Holy, Holy, Lord God of Hosts! Heaven and Earth are full of Your glory! Noreen excels in the kitchen. She is a whiz. Will it be melon to start, with a slice of orange to squeeze over it, powdered ginger from the posh cruet with the shiny, silver top? Or grapefruit segments, with a glacé cherry the only sweetness contrasting with the tang of the fruit? Followed maybe by some of that tender Welsh lamb, mint sauce, roast and boiled spuds, fresh greens and gravy? Or by something from the 'salmon falls', 'the mackerel-crowded seas', even by mouth-watering plaice and chips from John's Fish and Chip shop down Marlborough Hill? I have more saliva in my mouth than Mrs O'Brien's dog. I can hardly wait. Just have to find my glasses.

DING... DING... DING... DING... DING... DING. The bell again. Twice thrice. Two Sanctuses. Must be something good on to eat today. I struggle with my cuff-links. Fiddly little yokes, so they are. Jacket on. For sweet, I hope it is Noreen's apple pie. Crusty pastry and clotted cream. You can practically taste the rich pasture through the cream, spring blossom in the apples, sunshine from the caramelised sugar. With any luck, Cecil will have bought a bottle of Spanish Sauternes as it is Saturday. That will put me in my seventh heaven. If it is not the apple pie, let it be lemon meringue with the meringue crisp and lightly browned, trifle with plenty of sherry, or rhubarb crumble and custard.

Down the stairs. They will not ring the bell again. From inside the dining room, they will be able to see my hand on the banister through the coloured panes of glass in the dining room door. I am not so keen on the cheese, though Noreen likes to put out Stilton, a bit of mild Cheshire, and, if she can get it, some of that French Brie. The flaky, cheese biscuits are too dry. Custard Creams are another thing. Cannot stop eating them. I have a terrible sweet tooth and I am always thirsty. Still, give me ginger beer to quench my thirst anytime rather than that old Skull Attack I drank a few days ago. I pass the creaking stairs near the bottom. Hand on top of the decorative banister post. Swivel around. Not too fast. Along the hallway to the dining room. Stumble. Nearly trip over the slightly frayed carpet. Cecil, Noreen and Sean look up because they think I am about to fall. It is my own fault. I cannot resist peering ahead to see if I can spot what we are having for our first course.

Sometimes I look through the ruby glass in the right hand panel. The scene inside is sumptuous. The family look like revellers at a Roman banquet, especially if the bowl of fruit is in the centre of the table. The bowl which they kept the goldfish in when they first had it. The poor fish died soon after they moved it into a proper tank. I think it missed the aroma of fruit. If I look through the blue pane on the left hand side of the door, it all looks revolting, however nice the food is. Eggs in mayonnaise look like a plate of bubonic plague. The soup is like ink. Bread and butter resembles sliced mould from a time-locked dwelling beneath Vesuvius. Cecil, Noreen and Sean look worryingly cyanosed.

I wave at Sean today through the blue window because I know I look alien to him, as he does to me. Try to make him laugh. He must sit still at the table. Learn his manners. That is quite right. He must learn how to conduct himself.

"The soup is getting cold, Pop," Noreen encourages me to enter.

They have waited for me. They always do. They would never leave me out. How can I ever repay them? A fine film has formed over the surface of the tomato soup as it has cooled. They have waited that long for me.

"Don't wait for me. Please... please, do start, Noreen, Cecil, Sean... all of yous."

Noreen picks up her spoon. We all follow. The soup is wonderful.

Cecil takes a sip of soup without breaking his intense study of The Daily Telegraph. He is always on top of current affairs. If an article particularly interests him, he goes very still. You can see his fingers tighten and he moves the page even closer to his face. When he reads something he disapproves of, he shakes the pages violently as if something unpleasant is stuck to them. It sounds like a shower of hailstones hitting the paper.

"I think we've forgotten something, haven't we?" Noreen looks discomfited.

"The salt and pepper are here, behind the fruit bowl," I offer helpfully. Noreen does not hear me. Cecil rattles his paper.

"Sean, can you tell us, I wonder?"

Sean clamps a hand to his forehead to show he is thinking hard. I can tell he is stumped. Wondering whether it is possible his mother has come to believe, as he does, that we should start every meal with a pudding.

"We forgot our grace before meals," Noreen says it like it is the most surprising thing she has come across for a very long time. "Cecil, would you mind lowering your newspaper so that we can say our grace together? Would you like to lead us, Sean?"

"Bless us, O Lord, and these Thy gifts, which we are about to receive from Thy bounty, through Christ Our Lord, Amen. And may God bless the hands that cooked this meal." Sean knows the last bit pleases his mother. She rewards him with a warm smile.

"And please, God, give me a lot..." I add.

"And me..." Sean laughs.

"Do you mind, Sean?" Noreen looks hard at me, not Sean, as she says these words. Cecil rustles his newspaper again. He knows from the tone of Noreen's voice that he needs to demonstrate support for her point of view, despite not catching her actual words.

I suck my soup. They have immense soup spoons. Adhesion to the roof of my mouth is not so good at present. If I open my mouth too wide to gulp the soup, my top set comes adrift. Nothing stands still. Not even gums. So I stick to sucking. Noreen has been hinting for weeks that I should go to the dentist for a fitting to get myself a new set. I am about to bring this topic up when, on glancing towards Noreen, I notice an envelope beside the soup tureen. There is an Eire stamp on it. Is it my name? My heart accelerates. I wrote to Ireland as soon as Mammy died but got no reply. I had no address so I put Declan's name on it and sent it care of the Parish Priest in Bagenalstown. I wanted Declan, all of them, to come across if they could. None had met Mammy.

I wrote that Noreen and Cecil were offering to put the family up at the house. Not receiving any reply had not surprised me. I knew how they felt in Ireland about the 'Englishman' in the family who joined the British Army. I just thought, this once. For old time's sake. For childhood's sake. For Mammy's sake. I wanted Mammy to be given a dignified send-off. A fair crowd present to wish her well. I had hoped they might let the past go, after all this time.

The odd thing was that we had a visit about a month after I wrote to Ireland. The front door knocker took a hell of a hammering. It was a Friday evening about half past nine.

I hear Noreen's voice, "Is he expecting you?... And at this hour..."

Men's voices persist, cajole. There is the carefree, confident laughter of men in the prime of life. Men who usually get their own way. Finally, a note of intimidation creeps in. As if there is some urgency around. I hear Noreen's voice again, still indignant but obedient. Her footsteps ascend the stairs. I know her step so well. Behind her, there are much heavier footfalls. The tread of police, army personnel, men on a mission. They stop outside my bed-sitting room door.

"Pop, are you asleep?"

I keep as still as I can. A curtain is flapping in the breeze by an open window. The wooden curtain rings are clattering together. I stretch out an arm to hold the curtain still. A glass of soda water falls.

"Come on in, Noreen," I try to make my voice sound tremulous and weary, as if she has roused me from a deep reverie, "I was about to get settled for the night, but I am still awake."

"These gentlemen tell me they are from the Saint Vincent de Paul Society, Pop. They are visiting all the elderly parishioners.

The ones who have difficulty getting to Mass."

They have made at least one visit on their way to see me. I can smell the Guinness on their breath. There are three. Full of nods and smiles with Noreen in the room.

"I'll leave you to them then, Pop." Noreen glances uncertainly at the men. "Tea at ten," she smiles reassuringly at me.

The tallest man wears a heavy overcoat of herringbone weave. The thick cloth belt is knotted, no buckle – in the style of the old Chicago gangsters. Thick, black hair cloaks his head and brow. He has a packet of Sweet Afton in hand. He lights one. Does not do me the courtesy of asking whether I mind. Blows smoke rings. Lowers himself into the comfortable, reclining chair, near the bay window, where I usually sit. He has a quiet, threatening air about him, this one. His voice is soft, "So you are... er... Mr Connolly. Not related to the Mr Connolly I suppose, by any chance?" He is mocking me. He moves on to introductions, "They call me, Dermot."

The other two are Eamon and Patrick. They do most of the talking. Patrick explains, "They don't know us, you see. Your good daughter-in-law down below and her husband. We are just working in your Parish for the week. It is something the Saint Vincent de Paul Society like us to do. Visit each other. Keep the links going. En'tuse each other. They don't know us here, you see. So maybe they will listen to us more. All pulling together, but a little bit harder than usual. You could call it a kind of mission, I suppose, but we like to think of it as arms reaching out from across the sea."

Patrick is living proof that the Blarney Stone works. Must have a season ticket for the old castle there. He explains they all come from different Parishes in the South of Ireland and he himself, close enough, comes from Ballincollig. Just down the road from Blarney.

"What we are about is helping those that need it most, Mr Connolly." Cecil and Noreen's Parish Priest has given them a list of all the pensioners known to him in the Parish. They all realise how difficult it is, sometimes, when you are older, to get to Sunday Masses through the winter snow and rain.

Eamon takes over. Leans forward sympathetically, "The Parish Priest told us you do not seem able to make it down there too often, Mr Connolly. You have some difficulty, do you?" Eamon continues, almost too embarrassed to bring it up, "Said he had only met you the once."

Not wanting to put me on the spot further, Eamon goes on to describe their remedy. They are going to set up a Parish van and a rota of drivers to transport as many people as possible. It will all be organised so there will be nothing else needed to keep the arrangement going after they return home.

I pour them all a glass of soda water and a fresh glass for myself. I know what is coming. I tell them how good Cecil and Noreen are, "Really, really good. You know. Really... the tops." I mention how much easier it is for me to get to Church now Cecil has a little car. How he has not had it very long. How it has had a bit of mechanical trouble here and there. How fortunate we are in this house. Have a great deal to be grateful for. To thank God for, indeed. How Cecil and Noreen never fail to pass on to me their copy of the Catholic Herald. Weekly church notices. Invitations to coffee mornings for the African Missions. Details of proposed pilgrimages to Lourdes. Transcripts of the Archbishop's letters to the diocese. Appeals from the Parish Priest for donations towards the cost of the Church's new central heating system, new carpets for the Sanctuary, roof repairs and the training of extra priests. I convey, convincingly I hope, how well informed I am about Parish affairs. I tell myself that if I keep talking until ten o'clock, Noreen will rescue me with a cup of tea and they will go.

I have a terrible fear of going in a van with these men. Even for one Sunday, or any other day. I know not where they could take me. I walk slowly. I get giddy. I use a walking stick. Without knee-caps I would never walk again.

"Here's your night cap, Pop, as promised." Noreen manages to let my visitors know it is time to go, without being rude. She has regained her composure.

"You're an angel, Noreen, so you are. God bless you and save you." I ensure my language conveys an impression of god-fearingness to the men from across the sea. Whoever they are.

"They tell me, you are from the Mather Country... Mr Connolly." Dermot is crushing my hand in farewell,

"Bagenalstown... was it? Am I right? Was it Bagenalstown they told me?"

"That is where I was born."

"Bagenalstown... or... 'Muine Bheag' as we call it in Gaelic... 'Little Grove'... got a lovely poetic ring, hasn't it?"

"Mooeen Bag?"

"That's the ticket, Mr Connolly."

"Little Grove, you say?"

"Nicer than calling a place after that old Bagenal family, eh? I never met one of them in my time, did you... eh... eh... ha... ha... ha..!?"

"I did not... just so, just so, ha, ha, ha. I did not... no. That, I did not." I humour the man. He is clearly mad, dangerous, or both.

"A Carlow man, myself... 'Ceatharlach'... as we call it now, of course. 'The Four Lakes'... lakes lost in the mists of time... where the rivers Burren and Barrow join... the most lovely rivers in all of Ireland, don't you think, Mr Connolly?"

"I should say so. Without doubt, Dermot... the most beautiful... the fairest diamonds... from a great mineful through the country as a whole."

"Such a coincidence. Coming from the same part of the world... you and me... Mr Connolly." The man has hardly said a word all night and now he will not stop. What is he trying to tell me?

"An amazing coincidence, er... Dermot. By the way, what is your family name?"

"Pearse."

"It certainly rings a bell... but I don't remember knowing anyone..."

"The same stock, Mr Connolly, the same stock... even if we're not actually related. Nice to have met you. I will see you again... very soon." At last he loosens his grip on my hand.

I am trembling. My legs give way under me as I hurry to turn the flimsy key in my door. I throw myself sideways and land on my bed. The front door downstairs closes at last. They have gone.

Ten minutes later, when I am sure they are not standing outside the house, I call down to Noreen as quietly as I can...

43

"If those men call again, Noreen. Don't let them in please!"

They come back about a month later. The same heavy hand on the front door knocker. I have just finished listening to The Archers. Poor old Walter Gabriel has been in the wars as usual. Someone has plundered his vegetable garden, his winter greens are gone. Walter's prolonged groans and squawks of indignation merge with the signature tune at the end of the episode. There is time before bed to move over to my window seat for a few hours to watch the motor cars going up and down the hill, the mid winter horizon turning pink. It is just eight weeks since Mammy died. I still often sense her in the room with me. I like to imagine she is sitting quietly on the sofa behind me doing crochet work. She finished the woollen hearthrug, which now sits in front of the electric fire, shortly before she became ill. Endless patience went into it. Her trembling fingers lovingly worked every single strand of wool into the thousands of holes in that canvas base.

I hear Noreen open the front door. A few minutes later she comes into my room, "I told them you had a heavy cold, Pop. They left these for you." She hands me copies of the parish magazine and an envelope from the Parish Priest seeking donations for a new bus service being set up to ensure elderly parishioners can get to Sunday Mass.

The third time, a week after that, Dermot comes alone. I hear his quiet, authoritative tones undermining Noreen's defence that I am suffering from a migraine. "...for just five minutes, that's all I'm asking. It's still Church work we're on. We've had an extension. Your Parish Priest is so pleased with our work, he wants us to run the bus for a few weeks. Get it off the ground, like. I must just see Mr Connolly. It's really very important."

Noreen shows Dermot into my room. I notice a big bulge in the right hand pocket of his overcoat as he stamps across the room. He settles himself in the comfortable chair by the window like before.

"How are y', Mr Connolly?"

"Fit as a flea, as usual, Dermot, thanks. And how's y'self?"

"Noreen downstairs said yis had a migraine."

"Not for ten minutes since. It comes and goes like the weather, y'know."

"She said y'had it real bad."

"That's so, right enough," I start to understand what the Spanish Inquisition was like.

"Seeing you is a tonic in itself, Dermot. It raises my spirits no end." Dermot looks fractionally less suspicious. Sits further back in my chair.

"I'm sorry I can't stay with y'so long tonight... Mr Connolly. We're so busy. So much to do and so little time to do it. Eamon and Patrick have slipped up Victoria Avenue to have a chinwag with the widowed lady, Mrs O'Brien. I volunteered to visit you... as we share so much in common... while they are up there."

I hand Dermot a glass of fizzy limeade. He gulps it down in one. Suddenly he is across the room in one bound. Sits beside me on the sofa. Leans his head too close to mine. Stares at me fixedly, a wild look in his eyes. "It's a tough time for you... Mr Connolly. After so many years. Losing someone close. How long were you together?"

"Just over forty one years..."

"A mighty long time, sir. Will you pray with me?" Dermot's large hand is in the small of my back almost before his words are out. I am propelled off the sofa. I land on all fours. Struggle to a kneeling position.

"Eternal rest grant unto her, O Lord, and let perpetual light shine upon her. May she rest in peace..."

"Amen," I croak.

Dermot is up now and near the door. His right hand hovers above the bulge in his pocket. I shelter behind the bedstead hoping the mattress will absorb the force of the bullets in Dermot's unwieldy Browning pistol. His hand is in and out of his pocket in a flash.

"Take this... Mr Connolly." He hurriedly sets down a large wooden plaque on the mantelpiece, totally obscuring one of the mandolin players. "It's a little thing I carved myself. From one of Yeats's poems. Easter, 1916...

'MACDONAGH AND MACBRIDE
AND CONNOLLY AND PEARSE

45

NOW AND IN TIME TO BE,
WHEREVER GREEN IS WORN,
ARE CHANGED, CHANGED UTTERLY:
A TERRIBLE BEAUTY IS BORN.'

...just to remind you of the old country... Mr Connolly. Our namesakes died for a great cause, eh, eh? Without the old Easter Uprising in Dublin I don't believe the English would ever have shifted their arses out of Ireland. What say you?"

"That's very, very kind of you, Dermot. I really am most honoured." I notice today, Dermot's upper lip is covered with heavy, black stubble. His top lip curls up, as if in a sneer, revealing an upper set of gleaming white tombstones.

He has something else to say, "I'm back to Carlow next week. But I'm back here again the week after. Can I collect anything for you? Pass on any messages? You know. Anything like that... anything at all?"

I do not know. I do not know how Dermot knows so much about me. Naturally the Parish Priest is where he got my name. Only met him the once, at Mammy's funeral. The name of the small village I came from? Hardly anyone knows that. Dermot seems to know more about me than he admits. As if, behind the outward friendliness, he is hinting... 'I know you... I know who you really are... Mr Connolly... Where do your loyalties lie now, my friend?'

One thing I know is there is never any rush about settling scores; plenty of time for mayhem, even in the towns and fresh, green meadows of my birthplace. I just want to take life as it comes. Forget the flags. Walk the earth in freedom. I love the land of my birth and my adopted country.

Dermot has his hand on the doorknob.

"No thanks, Dermot. Nothing at present. I will let you know if I do. I haven't heard from them in Bagen... er, Muine Bheag for quite a while."

"Suit yerself,... Mr Connolly. Incidentally, I was wondering what your son, Cecil, does for a living? He's with them Civil Service Catholic Guild people I see."

"That's right. He's in the Civil Service."

"What sort of Civil Service would that be then? Employment, Tax, Immigration or what?"

"He works for the government. That's all I know. He doesn't say a lot about it."

Dermot finally takes his leave. He wants to know everything. What is Cecil's business to him? I take down Dermot's wooden plaque off the mantelpiece. Put it in one of Mammy's empty hat boxes under my bed. Next to the one I keep my night-time chamber pot in.

Noreen, Cecil and Sean have finished their first course. In silence, I finish mine.

"Slurp, slurp," Sean imitates the sound I make drinking my tomato soup.

"Silence, Sean," Noreen would not allow any disrespect for all the world.

I will empty my plate although I feel full. Noreen likes us to eat everything up. The helpings would satisfy a far younger, more active man than myself. I talk, to allow what I have eaten to go down, "Beautiful soup, beautiful soup. You're an ace with the tureen, Noreen, so y'are."

Noreen is scraping breadcrumbs into a brass scoop, "Some more, Pop? Plenty left..." She raises the tureen lid invitingly. Generous to a fault, that girl.

I pause. Give it lengthy thought. Decline. Notice again the letter from Ireland leaning against the soup tureen, "Whose is the letter, Noreen?"

"Yours, Pop. Came second post."

I become breathless. My ears ring. My heart beats fit to burst. I do not open the letter straightaway. Cannot hold the family up any longer. They are hungry. I rush through the rest of my soup.

Sean points solemnly at my face, "You have given yourself an orange moustache now, Grandad... Just like Daddy's."

"Take the soup plates into the kitchen, Sean, please," Noreen cannot scold Sean again. He has spoken so earnestly.

In between courses, I open the letter. I would recognise Declan's handwriting anywhere. Even after all these years. The large lettering, painstakingly fashioned, with curly flourishes on the capitals. His address is Gleann Bheatha Farm, Muine Bheag, Carlow. My big brother, Declan, is a farmer.

I hear Declan's words ringing down the years, "I am going to get me own farm when I am older. Just watch me." We are helping with the haymaking at Mary McDonagh's father's farm. Taking a breather. Surrounded by fields covered in liquid gold. Leaning on pitchforks. Sweating.

The custom was for local farmers to work together at each of their farms in turn, to get the hay in quickly. Village lads like us would join in for the fun of it and for the meal at the end of the day.

"Look at him..." Declan nods to where Mary's father is working. A forlorn figure. Bent over. The weight of a pitchfork pulling him down. Hands calloused and arthritic. Puffing and blowing he strains hard to keep up with the other men. "...His poor wife dead from T.B. and only Mary to help him on the farm." Declan looks grim, "I don't want to go grey before my time, as he has. He slaves his guts out night and day, and for what? To put rent into the pocket of a bastard landlord who does not give a fig for McDonagh's farm, or for McDonagh and his family."

The cart horse stamps and rattles in its harness, in the late morning heat. "Steady, Declan," I put my arm around his shoulders. Guide him back towards the others, "McDonagh is not worried about all that. He just wants us to help him get his blessed hay in."

"I swear to you, my closest brother. Things will change in this country before my life is through." Declan digs his fork deep into the hay. Swings it up onto the cart which will carry it to the barn for storage. His chest muscles ripple like the waters of the River Barrow, deep and strong. Mr McDonagh's barn will be full before the rain comes. Declan shifts as much hay as three men together. As I strive to emulate him, I see Mr McDonagh watching Declan, admiration and gratitude in his rheumy eyes, beyond expression in words.

Dust is everywhere. Hay moves along the chain of men. The cart is piled higher and higher. Words dry up as a rhythm sets in. An occasional grunt of effort. In the background, the gentle buzz and hum of summer. Hot sun on our heads. The older men use white handkerchiefs, a knot tied in each corner, to protect themselves.

"Our land is rich," Mr McDonagh becomes increasingly cheerful as he sees the work is progressing well. "There will always be enough bread and meat for everyone, thanks be to God. We have good soil, good crops,... good people. Thank you friends... Thank you." As Mr McDonagh scoops a few more strands of hay onto his devilishly heavy fork, the Church bell rings out. A strident, repetitive note. Twelve o'clock. Work stops for The Angelus. We kneel to pray, wherever we find ourselves; on the brittle stubble, beside the horse, at the top of the hay in the cart. Hats, handkerchiefs, are removed. Heads are bowed, hands clasped together.

Mr McDonagh leads us, "THE ANGEL OF THE LORD DECLARED UNTO MARY..."

In unison, we respond, "...AND SHE CONCEIVED OF THE HOLY GHOST."

Together we chant, "Hail Mary, full of grace, the Lord is with thee. Blessed art thou amongst women and blessed is the fruit of thy womb, Jesus. Holy Mary, mother of God, pray for us sinners now, and at the hour of our death."

Mr McDonagh peers heavenward, "BEHOLD THE HAND-MAIDEN OF THE LORD..."

We look up, as if to catch her words,... "BE IT DONE UNTO ME ACCORDING TO THY WORD."

Again, we recite, "Hail Mary, full of grace, the Lord is with thee. Blessed art thou amongst women and blessed is the fruit of thy womb, Jesus. Holy Mary, mother of God, pray for us sinners now, and at the hour of our death."

Piously, Mr McDonagh lowers his gaze to earth, "AND THE WORD WAS MADE FLESH..."

We rejoin, "...AND DWELT AMONGST US."

For the third time we chant, "Hail Mary, full of grace, the Lord is with thee. Blessed art thou amongst women and blessed is the fruit of thy womb, Jesus. Holy Mary, mother of God, pray for us sinners now, and at the hour of our death."

Mr McDonagh beseeches, "PRAY FOR US, O HOLY MOTHER OF GOD..."

"...THAT WE MAY BE MADE WORTHY OF THE PROMISES OF CHRIST," we add.

The prayers come naturally. We have been able to recite them without thinking all our lives. Imbibed with our mother's milk.

Mary McDonagh appears bearing pitchers of water, soda bread, cheese. The men drift into the shade to eat and drink.

"Would you like a look around the farm, Mr Connolly?" Mary asks me.

I blush as Declan and the other men look in my direction, grins on their faces. Mr McDonagh looks away, busies himself feeding a bag of oats to the horse.

"I would that, Mary. If you've time..."

She leads me down a foot-track between tall hedges, echoes of the men's voices, mimicking me, ringing in my ears... "if you've time! If you've time! So polite, the boy..."

"Don't mind them," Mary takes hold of my hand. Interlaces her fingers with mine.

"I don't... No... Not at all." My voice sounds lighter than usual.

"So... what would you like to see, Mr Connolly?"

"Oh, I don't mind at all. Whatever you like, Mary."

"I will take you down by the pond, then. There's plenty of shade there."

Mary wears a long black skirt which she hitches up with her other hand, to stop it dragging on the ground. Tucked into the skirt, a white lace-fronted blouse. Nothing on her feet.

The pond looks very deep. Its surface iridescent. In its shadowy depths sunbeams are diffused, absorbed, mingle with the sky's cobalt image, shatter in glittering star streams. Huge oaks and dense undergrowth screen it entirely. We scramble through to reach the pond's edge. Delicately, Mary removes loose leaves from my shoulders.

"Are you tired at all?" She leans her head on my shoulder, staring dreamily into the water.

"I am so, Mary. That hay-making takes it out of you a bit. I could do with a little nap."

"Will we lie down here a little while, then?" Mary stretches out on the bank, dangles one hand in the pond. I am beside her. We are kissing. Her cool neck. Her delicate ears. Her full lips. We press our mouths together so tight we can hardly breathe. I open mine wider, curl my tongue along the inside of Mary's top lip. Trace the delicate central tendon. "That tickles, Connolly." Mary squirms away from me.

"Will I stop it, will I? Don't you like tickles, Mary?" I tickle her sides. Under the arms. We roll over and over, away from the pond. A curtain of weeping willow covers us. Mary's skirt works up, above her waist. Her jet black bush contrasts mysteriously with the marble-whiteness of her thighs, her tightly curved belly. Impetuously I stroke between her legs in wonder and uncertainty, feeling like a small child. It is soft there, moist. Like the skin my tongue stroked inside Mary's mouth when we kissed.

"Just a minute, young man. Is the tickling over?" Mary grasps my wrist decisively.

"If you say so, Mary," I reply, afraid I have given offence.

"Then let me help you, Connolly." Mary pushes me down gently, onto my back. Her dexterous fingers unbuckle my old leather belt, slowly unbutton each of my fly buttons. The firm pressure of her fingers against me, as she twists the buttons through the button holes, rouses my Peetee as he has never been roused before. I am unaware of the damp, musty closeness of the earth, the air as pure and sweet as honey, the soapsud aroma on Mary's blouse, Mary's own warm scent. My consciousness takes it in without my knowing it. The scents are with me yet.

"Well, hello, young sir. Not so tired after all..."

Mary makes herself a starfish shape beneath me. I rest on extended arms, looking into eyes which harbour no fear, no doubt. Mary's mons veneris reaches up to accept me as I lower myself onto her. We fuse gently.

How long I rest there I will never know. Enclosed, at peace, more fulfilled than ever before in my life. Mary watches me patiently. I am afraid to move. My nerve endings are alight. I move slightly. Feel my pubic bone press down against Mary. She pushes back. Withdraws. Pushes back. I feel such a swelling surge of sweetness building up, I extend my arms, lever myself up and away.

"Bored... Already, Mr Connolly?" Mary teases.

"Aw, God, no. This is the happiest day of me life, Mary," I am aware of controlling a strong impulse to drive deep into Mary. To drive deep, to lose myself in an almighty explosion of creation. Through our melding, to nurture a seed of life, an atom of shared immortality.

"Hold tight, young man," Mary clasps me tightly between her

52

legs, encircles me in her arms, swivels neatly to her left, frees us from the weeping willow. She straddles me, her eyes glinting in the dappled sunlight. I could admire her there all day. Her hips move forward and back as if riding one of her father's horses. I relax. She slips her blouse off. Her breasts have lovely dark brown aureola around the nipples. I grip the nipples between forefinger and thumb. I do not know whether Mary will like it. I think of myself shelling peas, her nipples like peas bursting out from the pod. She moves on me harder. Whispers in time with her thrusts, "You... are... a... fine... han'some... lad,.. M'Conn'lly... I... knew... it... would... b'good... with... yoo... uuu."

"You are the best, Mary," I feel myself beginning to be swept down river in a flood of joyful letting go.

"We... are... vvv'... erry... good... to... gether... wouldn't... y'say?" Mary is excited, yet calm at the same time. My lips can no longer form words. I have to concentrate on other thoughts to calm myself. I imagine myself in a cavernous candlelit church, all alone. Still. Silent. I remind myself how my legs ache when I have to stand still for long periods on the altar. How hard the kneelers are when we are allowed to kneel. Under my breath, in rhythm with Mary, I begin to recite a soothing litany, like a mantra... 'Holy Mother of God... Pray for us, Holy Virgin of Virgins... Have Mercy on us, Mother Most Pure... Have Mercy on us, Mother Most Chaste... Have Mercy on us, Mother Inviolate... Have Mercy on us, Seat of Wisdom... Have Mercy on us, Cause of our joy... Have Mercy on us, Spiritual Vessel... Have Mercy on us, Mystical Rose... Have Mercy on us, Gate of heaven... Have Mercy on us.' It works. I hold on, unwavering, almost tranquil.

Seeing me calm encourages Mary to greater exertion. She steps up from a canter to a trot. She must ease back. I grasp her bouncing cheeks with both hands to slow her.

"Steady, Mary. Steady."

Mary is galvanised into a kind of frenzy by my touch.

"Don't stop me, don't stop me..." she gasps.

Her buttocks slide up and down against my hands. They are smoother and softer than chamois leather. I think to soothe her by stroking her tail with a very gentle, very light touch, to bring her back down to earth. She goes even faster. Her chin goes up, her neck extends, "Oh, yes, yes," she cries out laughing.

My thighs begin to tense beyond endurance, "Let's be careful, Mary," I groan, "We don't want y'to conceive or anything."

"Let's not stop yet," she moans in a deep voice I have not heard her use before.

"Queen of Patriachs, Pray for us," I shout.

"Wha'...?" Mary hardly pauses.

"Virgin most faithful, Pray for us," I yell.

"Go, go... oohhh... go!" Mary likes the shouting.

"Comfort of the Afflicted, Pray for us," I trumpet, almost allowing myself to lose concentration.

"Holy Mother of God, Connolly. What a cock y'have... Yes, yes... YES... "

We lie side by side. A starling sings a sweet song on the weeping willow. The giant oak trees' leaves have a misty sheen around them. I am so keyed up, I could fly to the top of the tallest. I breath deeply. One of Mary's arms lies haphazardly across my chest. I stroke the soft black hairs which cover her forearm from wrist to elbow.

"You weren't at all bad, Connolly," she murmurs, "We'll keep practising, will we?"

"I've not met anyone like you before, Mary,"

"Have y'not?"

"Are you not afeard of having a baby?"

"Babies are what nature intended, Connolly. Sure fucking is the most natural thing in the world. Doesn't The Bible itself spend pages telling us who begat who?"

"That figures though, Mary... come to think about it."

"Abraham begot Isaac; and Isaac begot Jacob; and Jacob begot Judas, and his brethren; and Judas begot Phares and Zara of Thamar; and Phares begot Esron; and Esron begot Aram; and Aram begot Aminadab; and Aminadab begot Naasson; and Naasson begot Salmon; and Salmon begot Booz of Rahab; and Booz begot Obed of Ruth..."

"How do you remember so much, Mary?"

"Me father likes us to read The Bible together in the evenings. He got very devout after me mother died. It gave him great consolation."

Mary springs to her feet, wriggles free of the skirt which still encumbers her middle, slides into the pool. I follow her in and hold her close. The coolness of the water is a great relief. Her wet skin is as smooth as glazed china. She slips through my arms. Swims away under the water to the bank.

As we return to the haymaking, we hear the low rumble of men singing. Someone is using the side of the haywagon as a makeshift drum. A simple beat. Thump. Thump. One. Two. One. Two. A slow marching song. Suggesting a monolithic advance.

"Up goes the shout
The guns are out..."

"What do you make of it all, Mary?" I want today to last forever. For nothing in the world to change in case it changes my world.

"I think something has to give, Connolly. People are tired of the promises. They don't believe them any more."

One of my arms is around Mary's shoulders. One of hers encircles me, her fingers resting lightly, so lightly, against my hip.

"Muster, men,
Fight for freedom
'Gainst the cruel
And vile foe..."

I can picture the men in my mind's eye, only a few fields away from us; smiling carelessly in the midday heat, urging each other on, heedless of consequences, brave in the isolated field, not thinking of the costs of their words in action. I do not believe they mean literally what they sing, anymore than they meditate on the meaning of The Angelus. Our village is too small for outside events to affect us overmuch. People like Mr McDonagh turn a deaf ear, want no more pain and disruption in their lives. Things are discussed. That is as far as it goes. People are aware of the issues. We know about absentee English landlords. We know Protestants are different from us. Father Michael has explained that only Catholic people go to Heaven.

"So, we'll not be seeing any Protestants up there, when we get there, if... we get there, my dear people," Father Michael

always says this with a leer, half humorous, half vampire imper-
sonation. He tells us to treat with contempt Protestant claims
that Roman Catholics are idolators, socially inferior people, who
go to Hell when they die. "We are all human. Catholics love
everybody. There is no need for good people who are not
Catholics to go to hell. Oh, no. They will be happy in a place
called 'Limbo', after the sins which stain their souls at the time
of their death have been purged in the cleansing fires of
Purgatory. God is fair about these matters. It would not be fair
to be sent to Hell for all eternity, just because you have not been
baptised a Catholic. Think of the unfortunate areas of the world
which the Catholic missions have not yet reached. The people
living in those areas don't know they should worship Jesus. Sure
it's not their fault."

"Life is too short to let bitterness and hatred poison our
lives." Father Michael stresses this when he meets the parents
of the handful of Protestant children who enter our junior
school each year. We learn, by mixing with them, that
Protestant children are just like everyone else except that they
neither have to attend Religious Instruction lessons nor Holy
Mass. They can read books, play games, do whatever they want
to do at these times, which causes a certain amount of envy
among the other children. Some of the very poor Catholic children, who cannot even afford boots, pick on the Protestant
children now and again, as if they need the consolation of
making someone else even unhappier than themselves.

O'Reilly's younger brother, Kieran, is the smallest child in the
junior school, apart from one of the Protestant boys. He often
takes hold of the Protestant lad around the neck after school.
Shouts at him, "Y'dirty Prod... Y'dirty Prod." No-one ever
moves to intervene. It all seems quite natural. There are so
many Catholics in the school. So few Protestants. The
Protestants do not matter so much, have no way to object.
Kieran is not noted for his knowledge during Religious
Instruction classes but of one thing he is sure, "Y'know where
you are after goin' when you die... DON'T YA?"

"No, I don't," the little lad blubs.

"Y're goin' to hell, so y'are... HELL."

There is one Englishman who lives just outside the village.

His nickname is 'The Major'. He lives alone in a cottage buried in a small wood, his only company a spaniel dog. He is seen outdoors rarely. When forced out to buy supplies, or exercising his dog down quiet country lanes at dusk. Everyone says he is an English spy. He must be a very lonely man. I find him friendly on the rare occasions I encounter him. I make a point of greeting him effusively, "Good day to you, Sir. A fine day today, don't you think?" The Major always looks up, stares me briefly in the eye, nods curtly. For a fleeting moment his mask slips. Deep crevices and creases appear in his face. I am never sure what that expression signifies. It reminds me how people sometimes say of others, 'If he smiled, his face would crack.' I think The Major is trying to smile. His spaniel has other ideas. Goes for my ankles. Snarls. Wills The Major to let him off the leash. "There, there," says The Major, "Don't fret. The young man means no harm." From his pocket he produces a tasty tit-bit. The dog is pacified. The encounter over.

"...And smash them
Like a thunderbolt..." In the field they sing on. An ominous dirge. Building themselves into a mood of heroism. I know Declan would no more fire a shot in anger than miss his Easter duties. The men are just feeling proud of themselves after a hard morning's work. They know they are going to get the job done and can relish the prospect of a good drink and repast later on at Mr McDonagh's table. Still the words are harsh, violent. They are playing with fire. I have seen the effect of prejudice on a small scale at my school. I do not want to see more of it.
"Muster, men,
For Emmet..."
And revolution thrives on the blood of martyrs.
"...Hanged high
In Dublin town."
As we sit around the huge oak dining table that evening, Mary brings out mounds of floury, white-fleshed potatoes bursting out of their skins, crisp pork, buttered cabbage and sparkling water drawn fresh from the pump. I try a little conversation with Mr McDonagh, "It's a fine farm y'have here, Sir."

"We count our blessings. Yet it takes much work to get a sufficient yield." He looks exhausted. Later, he produces three jugs of poteen. No-one sees where they come from. The conversation gets more and more lively. As the poteen disappears, the vigorous men of a few hours ago become slow and lethargic. Alone among them, Declan still sits with head held high, alert. I see his look stray in Mary's direction, as she busies herself with dishes at the sideboard. His eye lingers on her youthful form. I detect an interest there which he cannot conceal. He quickly averts his gaze as Mary returns to the table.

I have not thought of Declan's vow to own his own farm since that time. From his letter I see his prophesy has been fulfilled. I rejoice for him and turn to my son.

"Cecil, Cecil. Your uncle, Declan, has written to me... After all these years... And you know what?... He owns his own farm."

"Well, well?" Cecil looks over the top of his newspaper. Spots Noreen serving out perfectly browned lamb chops, mint sauce made with mint from the back garden, new potatoes, broccoli. He is understandably distracted.

I read parts of the letter aloud for all of them to hear. "Declan apologises for the delay in replying to me. You remember I wrote care of the Parish Priest because I didn't know Declan's address? Well, apparently, the Parish Priest put my letter in his back pocket meaning to pass it on to Declan... then forgot all about it. The housekeeper found it eventually... when the Parish Priest put the trousers out for washing. He was mortified, naturally... by then it was too late, of course. Declan got my letter a week ago and has replied straightaway."

"The Parish Priest doesn't put his trousers out for washing very often, then," Noreen is great on practical matters, "Mammy's been dead six months!"

"Declan says they would love us to go and visit them. It would give them unbounded pleasure to meet you all. Unbounded pleasure! Well, isn't that marvellous... Would you believe it, Cecil?"

"Ssshhh... Ssshhh... Quiet now. It's the one o'clock news coming up. Let's hear it." Cecil listens intently to the radio, continues to read The Daily Telegraph, and forks minted lamb, potatoes and broccoli into his mouth, all at the same time. How he does it, I do not know. His brain must be enormous.

"Pip, pip, pip, pip, pip, pip... Here is the one o'clock news."

"H'eah ez tha wan o'clack newsa," Sean attempts an imitation of the announcer's Oxford English.

"Sean, your father needs to listen to this. He has to know

about these things for his job." Noreen puts her hand against her mouth indicating Sean should do the same.

"First a report from our Labour Correspondent... 'A claim for a substantial increase in wages for farm workers was presented at a meeting of the Agricultural Wages Board yesterday. The National Union of Agricultural Workers are seeking a new minimum wage of about eight pounds a week – an increase of nineteen shillings'..." Cecil rattles his paper unhappily at this news. We hear him comment, "Don't know why... Live in lovely free cottages... usually. In the countryside. Fresh air. Outdoors... what more do they want?"

Cecil's description of the agricultural workers' conditions of work reminds me of a question I have been meaning to ask.

"I was wondering, Cecil, what exactly does your job involve? A man asked me a little while back and I realised I didn't know. I hope you don't mind me asking."

"Please... Ssshhhh." Cecil cranes closer to the fabric square where the sound crackles out of the radio.

"I'm so sorry. I forgot you were listening to the radio, Cecil."

"...In the past year foot-and-mouth disease, brought in meat from South America and by birds from the Continent, has proved a costly affliction to our stock breeders and taxpayers. Discussions have been proceeding with the Argentine authorities to stop the spread of the disease in this country. Last Thursday, in the House of Commons, the Parliamentary Secretary to the Ministry, Mr Godber, stated that it is important to make clear to South American countries that if they want to continue to enjoy the use of the British market they must be able to give their produce a clean bill of health. It was acknowledged there is nothing we can do to stop birds from crossing the Channel from France, but we should urge the French authorities to use fully every modern means, such as the vaccination now practised in Continental countries, to check the course of the disease when it appears."

"The Official Secrets Act..."

I do not see Cecil's mouth moving because I am tucking into my second helping of broccoli when I hear these words, but it is he who has spoken. His newspaper shields him from direct view.

"I cannot discuss my job... Official Secrets Act." It is definitely Cecil speaking. I recognise his voice.

"I understand, Cecil. Absolutely. You can't argue with that. It'd be more than your job's worth to breach that... and you've got a wonderful little job there, too. Whatever it is you do."

Cecil's silence serves to underline his acquiescence with my comments. The news is drawing to a close.

"...And our final item, this lunchtime. The rule that there should be no talking by prisoners working in prison workshops has now been relaxed. In a recent circular the Prison Commission states that in future prisoners will be allowed to talk to each other, provided there is not excessive noise, that good order is maintained, and that output is not affected. Talking during exercise periods has been allowed in British prisons since 1939.

That is the end of the news."

"And now the news from Ireland," I announce.

"Is it really, Grandad?"

"No, Sean. It's Uncle Declan's news. I'll read you some more, shall I?"

"If you want to, Grandad."

"Declan and his wife, Mary, have five children."

A knife pierces my heart for a moment. Mary? Mary McDonagh? He does not say.

"Declan and she would particularly like their children to meet their English cousin, Cecil. How about that Cecil?"

I would die happy if I could only see Mary again. To say farewell. I must not build up hopes. He could just as easily have married a girl from Carlow, from anywhere in Ireland. Half of the women in Ireland are called Mary anyway. And even if it was Mary McDonagh he married, we are all different people now. A whole lifetime's experience separates Mary and me from our short days of closeness. Yet I would love to meet her again and I will never know who Declan married unless we go over to visit. I could never ask a question like that in a letter.

"Well, what do yous say? Eh? Cecil... Noreen... Sean... Will we go across for a visit to Ireland?" I know I would not be up to travelling on my own. Please God make them say 'yes'.

"Yes, please. I would like to ride a horse, Grandad."

"Sean. Your great Uncle Declan will let you ride on ten horses. I'll make sure of that for you."

"It might be interesting?" Cecil looks enquiringly at Noreen.

"It would certainly be educational for Sean..."

"We could take him to see The Book Of Kells and The Book Of Durrow." Cecil looks suddenly interested.

"...and we do have the car now. It would be a nice little holiday for all of us." Noreen is a great believer in the restorative value of short breaks.

"Hooray," shouts Sean loudly, despite being the least well informed about the business in hand. I think he senses the restrained excitement in all of us. In me for obvious reasons. In Cecil, at the prospect of viewing Irish historical sites and monuments in abundance, and at meeting living evidence of his own family history. In Noreen, because she will be able to expand Sean's knowledge with a visit to a new country.

"I will make the necessary arrangements for the ferry journey. We shall travel at the start of the school holidays," Cecil declares decisively. He will take care of everything.

How marvellous. To see Ireland again. Visit all the family still living there. Meet their children and grandchildren. Step on Irish turf owned by a Connolly. Something I never ever expected to be able to do. All these wonderful things sparked off by the tragic loss of Mammy. How she would have loved to make this journey with us.

The last time I was in Ireland was in my fifteenth year. I find myself with time on my hands. I have left school with the School Certificate. A young man with fine copperplate handwriting and no job. I cannot hang about the house all day. I am out helping the farmers, giving my parents any pocket money I earn to help support the family, reading whatever books I can beg, steal or borrow, lying in the sun on the riverbank, sheltering under trees through the showers. Wise Lucretius salves my frustrated desires for a while. Reminds me of the joy of being in a quiet sanctuary. Dismisses futile striving for wealth and power. Idealises the simple pleasure of reclining on soft grass by a running stream under the branches of a tall tree, refreshing one's body pleasurably at no expense. But to base one's existence on avoidance of appetite is a hard road to follow for a young man, however much calm spirit it engenders.

I cannot help wanting to make something of myself. I want to spend my life with Mary but I do not expect her to want me unless I am established, can offer her security in a few years time. If having love only results in a desire for more love – so be it. I will accept the turmoil. I will follow Lucretius's ideas when I am older, if they suit me then.

One empty day I read in the weekly newspaper they are recruiting at the barracks in Curragh, County Kildare. My problem is solved. The Army offers a good career, security, travel, adventure. A life to offer Mary. I wonder how she will like me in a uniform. I might get to be an officer after a few years.

My family are opposed to it. What hurts most is my father's reaction, "You'll not set foot in this house again if you join that infamous army of oppression. You'll be no son of mine."

It is my decision. My mind is made up. Mary does not mind me joining up but says she would prefer it if I stay. She does not care about careers and all that squit. She promises she will wait for me. Will join me when the time is right. I want to take her out of Ireland, somewhere she can live free of worry about the future.

One of the saddest days of my life is a bright, sunny Friday. All the family, except my father, crowd into our tiny front garden as I get aboard the pony and trap to drive the thirty miles or so to Curragh. They cluster together like a living organism from which I have been torn away, become detached. They look at me curiously now. Impersonally. A familiar part of their emotional landscape has inexplicably become unrecognisable. They wave half-heartedly, "Take care, then," "See yous soon," like I am just going for a gentle drive to Carlow and back. Just as I am moving off, Dominic, my brother who became a priest in Nigeria, steps forward and presents me with a brown scapula to wear around my neck. "Wear this at all times. Remember, Our Lady promised that whoever dies clothed in the brown scapula shall not suffer eternal fire." I thank him.

I stop off at the McDonagh's farm to say goodbye to Mary. She has been in the kitchen baking shortbread. Puts her arms around me. Holds me tight. I squeeze her against my ill-fitting tweed coat. We both know it will be some time before we meet again. Our embrace expresses silently what we are feeling. I think of it now as love. Mary hands me a parcel of shortbread to take with me. I leave quickly. Wave at the curved figure of Mr McDonagh in the distance. I do not think he recognises me. He slowly raises an arm in reply. I take it as a blessing.

At the Curragh barracks they strip us down to our underwear. Get us to fill lots of forms. Cut our hair. Put us in uniforms so we all look the same. I lie about my age to get accepted. We are made to drill until we lose count of the blisters on our feet. I lose track of the days. I remember one particularly hard day lying on my bunk in the dormitory, staring at the corrugated ceiling of the hut, thinking 'who am I?', 'will I ever come through this?'. Deep down I never lose a certainty that I will come through. I have the future with Mary to look forward to.

We are sent for more training to Wiltshire. The countryside is lovely but in the background there is the continual crump, crump, of the big guns rehearsing for war.

Mary and Declan are the only ones who write from home. Declan only once or twice. He was never one for much book learning. Mary writes at least twice a week; about her life on the farm, how she is missing me, how she hopes I think about her all the time. She puts pressed flowers in with the letter with a note to say they are from the banks of the pond where we spent so many happy hours. The exclamation marks make me laugh. After a few months the letters stop. A final letter comes through from Mary. She explains her feelings for me have not changed. She will come to me whenever I am ready. She is finding it difficult writing me letters without seeing me between times. I write back to say that I understand. That I will not write again until I am in a position to offer her a home. I hope it will be soon. I put her letter, with all her other letters and the brown scapula, in the compartment in my suitcase for holding valuables. That letter is still in the old suitcase. I have never thrown it away.

Noreen serves giant portions of apple pie and clotted cream. It melts in your mouth. I eat half without stopping. My stomach suddenly tells me to rest. There is more of Declan's letter to read but I put it away to finish off quietly in my room. It is enough that Cecil has agreed to make the trip. His first to Ireland. The thought of returning there increasingly fills me with excitement and... sadness. So many farewells were never properly said. It is strange to contemplate returning, as if I am coming back from a few hours drive to Carlow – so little have I shared with them of my life since I left.

"Anything wrong with the pie, Pop?" Noreen is beginning to look hurt.

"Noreen, Noreen. I want to tell you something about the pie... in confidence!" I love to joke with Noreen. Even more because she is such a serious minded person. I hold my desert spoon face down. Place it across the top of my tea cup. She has the best china out because it is the weekend again. I hold the tip of the spoon handle and jerk it up and down. 'CLANK CLINK CLANK CLANK CLINK CLINK CLANK CLANK CLANK CLANK CLANK CLANK CLINK CLANK CLANK CLINK CLANK CLANK CLINK CLINK CLINK CLINK.' The fine china is definitely best for Morse Code. It gives a lovely ring to the signals.

"Come on, now, Noreen. What would you say that means?"

"No idea." Noreen is not trying.

"Let's try it again then. See if you catch it this time." She usually guesses wrong. But we all have a good laugh about it. Noreen is a real sport. 'CLANK CLINK CLANK CLANK CLINK.'

"O.K. O.K., Pop. It means 'Good Afternoon'."

"No, no. Ha ha. Miles out. MILES out. Come on. Guess again. Stop me with a guess, stop me..." I am getting the rhythm just right. My old sergeant would be proud of me. 'CLANK CLINK CLANK CLANK CLINK...' Noreen's face is hardening. She is really stumped this time.

"Righto. I'll tell yous... 'Yummy Pie'... that's what it means." A great thing military training. I can send a secret message anytime I want, "Yummy pie, Noreen. Eh? Thought you might get that one. It is too... truly delicious pie. Here, now. Try this one." I will give them an easier one this time. 'CLINK CLINK CLINK CLINK CLINK CLANK CLANK CLINK.'

"So what d'you think that was? Sean?"

"Bum," volunteers Sean.

"Thank you, Sean," Noreen glares at him.

"Incorrect, Sean. It was 'Sean'. Your very own name. How about that?"

"Will you teach me mouse code, Grandad?"

"Would you like your tea brought up to your room, Pop?"

"Waah? Oh, yes. Yes, Noreen. That's very kind of you."

Up in my room I begin to finish reading Declan's letter. I feel such joy that Cecil wants to visit the old country. He has never shown any inclination to go there in the past. I know he will love it. I used to try to describe for him the beauty of the Wicklow Mountains; Lugnaquillia Mountain, Mullaghcleevaun, Glendalough. It must have sounded like a never-never land to him, somewhere left far behind me on a long, irretraceable journey. He is so understanding, sensitive. He has never brought it up. Never asked about his uncles. Britain has been our home. He has been a real credit to me and Mammy. If you did not know he had an Irish father you would never guess.

Declan addresses me as his "closest brother". He could not say a kinder thing. So the paths of our lives diverged. We are still brothers. He describes his farm. A water pump outside. But running water inside the house now too. Electricity for the cooker. Himself and Mary in the present farmhouse, with their eldest son, daughter-in-law and three children. Crowded. Have nearly finished building a larger house higher up the hill. He and Mary may stay in the old house. Have it all to themselves for the rest of their retirement.

It all sounds wonderful. How valuable our families are to us as we get older. I do not know where I would be without Noreen and Cecil. This past winter since Mammy's death. I could not count the number of trips they have taken me on to take my mind off things.

They know I love the coast. One of our favourite destinations is Sully Island. So peaceful there. Lots of sea air. But a dangerous place. It is January. A Sunday. The worst Christmas of my life has passed, Mammy only buried five weeks before. There are no other cars in the small parking area. We clamber out. Huddle together. Take in the view. Dusk is settling over the landscape.

Cecil guides us through the main points of interest, in case they have slipped our memories since our last visit, "Over there is Sully Island." He realises the island is hard to miss, dominating the view, as it does, only three hundred yards in front of us. But he is thinking of Sean. So typical of him. He consults his watch, "The tide is coming in. It'll cover the rocks in three quarters of an hour. We'll have to get a move on, if we are going to get across and back today."

Between the shore and the island, there is a stretch of uneven, stratified limestone, just visible above the waves. It is covered in wet seaweed and a viscous green slime. The tide has always been in on our previous visits. A water droplet is building up at the end of my nose. It hovers there, trembling in the icy squalls gusting up channel.

"I think I'll just wait in the car, Cecil. If you don't mind." I will enjoy sitting for a while, thinking, watching the shipping inch its way through the sea mist, around the countless rocks, sand-banks, shallows and islets which throng the waters of the Bristol Channel.

Cecil agrees it makes sense for me to remain in the car, "Binoculars in glove compartment." He continues for Sean's benefit, "Over there are the Flat Holm and the Steep Holm islands. Where Norse raiders used to stay when pillaging this coast. The Flat Holm is the low lying one. The Steep Holm is..."

"The steep one..."

"Sean," Noreen knows Cecil does not like to be interrupted.

"...the one with high escarpments on all sides."

"Would that make it hard to land there?" Noreen looks admiringly at Cecil's profile.

"Yes, it certainly would... and I fancy that may be why there was a monastery there many centuries ago..."

"Well, well, well," Cecil's knowledge never ceases to amaze me. I have to remind myself he was a young man when he left Mammy and me to follow his Civil Service career. He has been developing for so many years since, training his mind. I think the secret is, he never lets up. Always takes his lunchtime snack to the reference library.

"...just ruins now, of course. On the Flat Holm there was an isolation hospital some time ago. For victims of smallpox..."

I spy another distant land mass. I have forgotten what Cecil told us it was last time. "Is that another island, Cecil?"

"Oh, no, no, no. Right over there... jutting out, that is Brean Down. That is England. Land of the free. A magnificent vista isn't it? The lights you can just see coming on to the left of Brean Down are in Weston-Super-Mare."

"That's seaside, isn't it?" Sean remembers the important things.

"Exactly, Sean... and note carefully the Roman associations within its name, Weston-Super-Mare. 'Super-Mare' is Latin, you see. It means Weston-Upon-Sea. So people must have been living in that region since Roman times. That is interesting isn't it?"

"Can I go swimming today, Dad?"

"Today? Ha, ha, ha. It's far too cold, son. Swimming! In the middle of winter!" It is nice to hear Cecil laughing. He has so little free time in which to relax.

I remember what lies beyond, hidden by Brean Down. Berrow Flats extend southerly as far as Burnham-on-Sea, where we were living when Mammy got ill.

"See yous later, then." The car is still warm inside. Cecil, Noreen and Sean step out briskly along the swiftly shrinking route to the island. Now I sit and look across to Burnham-on-Sea. Thinking of our life there. Our joys and sorrows. When Mammy and I lived there I also used to look out to sea. To the west. Knowing there was no land between me and Ireland. I always seem to have been searching for bits of myself over the horizon. Yet still I survive in one, moth-eaten, piece. I do not look back with regret. I acknowledge. Celebrate the hours I have drawn breath, walked on this beautiful earth.

The windows inside the car soon mist up. It becomes impossible to follow the family's progress. I hope they keep safe. Cecil has checked the times of the tides. It is essential to check. He discovered that the tide in this channel has the second highest rise and fall in the whole world. I wipe clear a window within a window. Find the binoculars. There is Sean. Rushing on ahead. Slipping and sliding on the rocks like a little ice skater. He seems not to feel the cold. Looks so smart in his school uniform. Bright red blazer. Golden braid. Peaked cap with school crest. Noreen and Cecil have him in an excellent Catholic School. Private, of course. Nearly one hundred per cent eleven plus pass rate. Some pupils are coached for the common entrance exam. Progress to big public schools like Stonyhurst and Ampleforth. He is being given a great opportunity. Will be able to converse on equal terms with anyone in the land. Noreen is calling after him. Telling him to keep his lovely uniform clean I bet. She is grasping Cecil's arm. Cecil's lips are moving. He points at the plentiful rock pools, probably describing the diverse wildlife within.

I wipe another space clear. Survey my surroundings. Trees and shrubbery bent double by fierce westerlies. A few caravans, closed up for the winter. One inhabited building. A restaurant. Not open at this hour. The Sully Inn. 'Very posh', Noreen calls it. Expensive too. She says a meal costs as much as three pounds, even without drinks. Says she could cook at home just as well for a quarter of the cost. Still I would treat them all to a slap up meal if I could afford it. They deserve it. I had no more life in me than a spent match, when I came to live with them.

I turn the binoculars in the direction of the island. There is no sign of any of them. Neither on the rocks. Nor on the island. I fear for them. Have they slipped in? Been washed away in rip currents? The only thing visible is the wooden frame of an old ship-wrecked lugger, buried beneath heaps of rock and shingle.

I will be useless if they are in trouble. Cannot drive. Could not run to find a telephone. I get out of the car. Walking stick in one hand. Binoculars in the other. They are heavy. No hat. It would not stay on for long in this breeze. I see seagulls wheeling high above the centre of the island. Crying. High-pitched, excited squawks. Something is down there below them. A red smudge is moving along the top crest of the island. The smudge waves its arm above its head as if it has just been awarded top marks in a skating competition. It is Sean. Thanks be. But is he waving in distress? Is there something wrong? He seems to be waving at me. I lean against the car. Wave my walking stick in a wide, reassuring arc. Sean does not see me. I stagger, weakened by the unaccustomed effort. Get back inside the car. I know now how Captain Scott felt at the Antarctic. You feel so helpless. But I too shall stick it out to the end. There may be something I can do.

Cecil's head and shoulders appear as he ascends the far side of the ridge. Noreen's not long after. As they reach the top of the ridge I see Cecil is walking very fast. Not running. That would not be his way. Noreen is almost being dragged along. They must have got involved in looking around on the far side of the island. Shallow water is already flowing across parts of their way back to the mainland. They will be cut off by the tide. I can only watch. I think they should stay put but I have a feeling Cecil will not wait. He leads them forwards. I am going to lose them. Sean gets interested in a rock pool. He seems to be finding it all a great game. Is unaware of the danger. Cecil urges him on. The water is streaming over their feet, nearly covering their ankles. Sean soon discovers that stamping his feet splashes water everywhere. Noreen lunges forward to grasp his hand. Slips. Clutches wildly at Cecil. They are both down. In it up to their waists. They stumble forward. They cannot see where it is safe to step and blunder terrifyingly from shallow areas into deep pools and back again. Finally they reach higher, dry ground. Safety.

I cannot hide my relief at seeing them all safe and sound. I wind down the window and call out, "Thank goodness. You've made it. Sure, I thought I was to lose the lot of you for a minute there."

"Nothing at all to worry about. Everything was perfectly under control." Cecil must have nerves of steel.

They all join me in the car.

"It was all such f... f... f... f... fun, Grandad."

"Got your swim in after all then, Sean," I smile. You have to laugh at him.

"There's a marvellous view on the far side of the island, Pop. You would love it."

"Maybe one day in the summer, I'll come over with you, Noreen." Sully Island is one of our favourite spots. We have been back several times since.

Declan's letter has been a tonic and no mistake. What more could a fellow ask from life? A lunch fit for a gourmet, convivial company, and beside me on the sofa this letter from my long-lost brother. A brother who wants to see me. Wants to join together two family branches. After all these years. And a fresh cup of char arriving to boot.

Noreen places the cup and saucer beside me with care. She puts it on the plastic tray which is clamped onto the arm of the sofa. A handy little yoke it is.

"Do us a favour, Pop."

"Anything, Noreen... anything."

"Look after Sean this afternoon?"

"Tell the little man, 'Come up as soon as you like'."

"We've some last minute shopping to do for this evening..."

It is the least I can do. I pay a small sum towards my keep. They will not take much. I am not able to help a great deal. It feels good to be allowed to do any small thing. Even such an easy task as looking after my grandson for a few hours.

"Come on in... Don't wait out there." You would not normally expect a little one of seven to knock on a door in his own house. Great manners they teach him in that school of his. Sean settles down at the far end of the rug, away from the heat of the electric fire. Noreen has given him four or five books to keep him busy and his religious instruction homework to complete.

"Grandad...?"

"Sean...?" Sean is a stickler for asking questions at the present.

"I know Father Christmas doesn't exist, but there is a God isn't there?"

"God, Sean?" I try to sound vague. To imply I have not given it much thought.

"Our teacher says God is a big man. There are three of Him actually. And He lives in a little cupboard on the altar at church. In The Taptackle or something..."

"Tabernacle is the word, Sean."

"Yes... and I remember, Grandad, God has a Tabernacle in every church. He lives in His Tabernacles – they are God's houses... and when we take our First Holy Communion soon and swallow God's body down inside us – we will be God's houses too!"

"Ahhh..."

"And He is everywhere as well, at the same time..."

It is difficult for me to comment. Children's minds are so precious and Sean can always tell whether I am levelling with him. Things make such an impression when you are young.

I still recall a lay teacher we had at Recknaw College. Told us about Saint Thomas Aquinas's explanation of God's existence. Mister Everitt, the teacher's name. Sharp-featured. Piercing eyes. An exceptionally devout man. So intense in his belief. Always red inflammation around his nostrils and the skin on their outer edges. As if he breathed fire in private but was too discreet to do so in public. Maybe he just suffered from hay-fever.

"Who wants to be able to prove God exists? Hands up there. Let's see how many budding theologians we have. And don't ask me what 'theologian' means, O'Reilly, for God's sake..."

"To know Him, love Him and serve Him, Sir." O'Reilly has not been listening.

"That is the reason why God MADE you, boy... To know Him, love Him and serve Him in this life, and to be happy with Him for ever in the next. I cannot help thinking God had a bit of an off day when He made you, O'Reilly..."

When the unkind laughter has died down, Mr Everitt puts on his serious face, "Where did this earth come from? This solar system? This universe?"

"God made it, Sir." O'Reilly tries hard now to impress with keenness.

"Wrong again, O'Reilly. Leastways, it's not so simple as that. Now listen carefully. A lot of heretics say our universe is part of a bigger creation, that our Creator could have been created by an even more powerful being. Or they say that there was a big explosion and the world just appeared from a big ball of gas, and that the gas could have come from another bigger explosion before that, or that everything which we can see in space could be just like a speck of dust in a far bigger operation altogether. Clear?"

"Sirrr,.." we all chant.

"Imagine a row of skittles in a line, lads. Easy for you, O'Reilly. You're always at the beer and skittles, isn't that so?"

"Not at all, sir." O'Reilly looks all around the classroom as if he suspects his classmates of calumny.

"The furthest skittle falls against the one next to it. What happens?"

"You score two points, sir?" O'Reilly is less confident this time.

"Wrong for the third time, lad. Anyone?"

"They fall, sir," we all call out together.

"Yes... and... and...?"

"The second skittle knocks the third one down..."

"O'Reilly! We'll make a theologian out of y'yet, boy. Well done!"

"What is a theologian, Mister Everitt?"

Mister Everitt is already moving on, "So you've got that, class? The first skittle is God. However far one has to go back to the beginnings of everything. That is God. You will always be able to prove He exists now. The One True Catholic God..."

Mr Everitt left me visualising God as some kind of giant skittle for years after that. I assumed a lucky collision around the dawn of time had sent the skittles our way. I thought how fortunate we had been. Until it occurred to me that the process might not have ended. Were the skittles still falling? Started worrying. Could we topple anytime?

'I've been looking for God for fifty years. If I was going to find Him I think I would have done so by now.' George Bernard Shaw's words come close to describing my situation.

"...But no-one can see Him because He is infizzable?"

"Invisible."

"Yes, Grandad."

"You've remembered your lesson very well, Sean."

"But do you believe he is everywhere, Grandad?"

"I just don't know, lad. Cleverer people than me disagree about God."

"I prayed He would get me a bicycle for Christmas – and He did!"

"That was excellent."

"It was green though. Not the blue one that I wanted."

"Really?"

"Should I leave the colour up to Him next time?"

"You might as well. Sometimes though, things do seem

meant to be, don't they? As if someone is watching over us. Things work out. I remember how I felt when your Daddy was born. When you were born. When I used to cuddle and kiss your Granny. When you got back safe and sound from Sully Island that day!"

"The day I swam in the sea in January..." Sean springs to his feet to demonstrate his heroic escapade.

"When your Granny died I was very sad. Like God's attention had been distracted elsewhere. Things can go wrong if you neglect them even for a moment, can't they? Remember when you left your homework book out on the kitchen table and went to get one of your Mummy's angel cakes from the larder?"

"And next door's cat got in and knocked my bottle of ink all over it..."

"These things happen, Sean, to the best of us... we try to accept... Sure there's no need to worry your head about understanding everything yet. You've plenty of time."

"Righto, Grandad. But do dolphins and elephants and whales... and... animals... go to Heaven, like we do?"

"Ah. Now you are asking something important. They care a lot about each other. They hate to be parted, don't they? Noah had to make sure he had animals with him on the Ark... So..."

"I hope dolphins go to heaven..."

My eye strays to the window sill. Before Sean came in I could hear a frenzied buzzing. There is buzzing again. An angry sound. Then again, silence. A dead fly. On its back, beside two others. Sean does not notice.

Lucretius is sure where we came from. No doubts at all. He explains that when Mother Earth was new and even more fertile than she is now, human beings were incubated in cosy, moss-lined wombs underground. Watered and warmed by showers and the sun's rays, babies would come out when the time was ripe, to feed on sweet milk from veins in the land. As the Earth cooled and aged we had to adapt, developed the capacity for reproduction within our own bodies.

Lucretius's theory seems as plausible as anyone else's. So far as I can tell anyway. He tells a good yarn, with conviction, passion even. When we are gone, he says, nothing will have power to disturb our senses, not though earth be fused with sea and sea with sky.

I watch Sean writing in his book so seriously. The Jesuits used to boast, 'Give us a child's mind for the first seven years of life and it is the Church's forever'. I was born into it. But I do not belong to the Church. Could be the first person to prove the Jesuits wrong. To escape the years of mental moulding. I am a free thinker. But if I am free why do I spend so much time going over what I do not accept? Time and time again, measuring out my life with crucifixes. Everything still has to be compared to those decaying foundations clumsily laid in my childhood brain.

One person's joy is another's nightmare. Is little Sean finding a philosophy for life? Or being strapped into a straight-jacket? I wish I knew. Does sanctity like Ma O'Keefe's help preserve a fragile sanity? Or turn life into an unending flight from damnation?

"We're funny mortals, Connolly," she says to me strangely, pressing some coins into my hand as I mingle with the family and other parishioners after serving Mass.

"Speak for yourself," Declan mutters under his breath.

"We are that, Miss O'Keefe," say I, "God bless you." I think she sees me as a miniature priest because I am on the altar. Wants a closer bond with those closest to the celebration of the Mass. Finds me more approachable than the priests.

"You have lovely hands," she says haltingly, holding them a long time in her own as she passes me the money.

"If God made the world, Grandad. Where did he get it all from?"

I am tempted to refer Sean to Mr Everitt's skittles but have another thought.

"We know men and women could not have built it. No lorries big enough are there?"

"No, Grandad."

"And the earth, the moon and stars got where they are somehow."

"Yes, Grandad." Sean is jotting my comments down for use in his homework book.

"We have not even reached the moon yet. So human beings could not have made that either."

"So God must have found 'em somewhere and made his own arrangements at the time."

"That's a possibility alright, Sean."

"And that man in the moon. Is that God too?"

"Mebbe... and on the other, dark side of the moon, which we never see, could there be a lady in the moon too? A lady who helps God to look after us all. A Mammy God who cares about us even when the big Man God is busy. A Mammy God in charge of keeping people warm, encouraging them to love each other, not letting people suffer too much, cheering them up when they are sad, making sure there is help at hand when storms and floods wreck people's homes. How would that be?"

"Lovely, Grandad."

I do not think they will get to the moon for a few years yet. Not in my lifetime anyway. They keep talking about launching satellites to orbit the earth. I cannot see them managing it. Who knows? Maybe the answer will be there, somewhere out in space. Maybe it will be possible then to shed more light on the mystery of our existence. We are in such a strange situation. Big brains. We realise we are spinning ceaselessly, uncontrollably, around the sun, on a crust-covered molten mass. No information or knowledge to explain the purpose of living, beyond living itself.

Sometimes people convince themselves that they have the whole truth. Then everyone else must believe that same truth or the illusion of being in control of their own destiny, which knowing gives, is threatened. Galileo put forward his idea, that the earth moved around the sun, when everyone thought the earth was at the centre of things. Poor man was tortured, branded a heretic, told to retract. Did so.

As for myself. Not getting any younger. I must admit it. It would be such consolation to know that eternal happiness stretches ahead when I die. To be with loved ones again after I have gone. A beautiful thought, right enough.

If a bearded figure, bearing the golden keys to The Kingdom on his belt, floats forward to greet me as I pass away, I will own I have been mistaken. "A very, very good day to you, sir," I will say.

"Happy eternity," he may riposte, the words muffled by his flowing whiskers.

"Have I the pleasure of meeting Saint Peter?" I to him again.

"I can check if he's in," he to me.

"Just tell him, please," I may be getting a bit anxious here. "It was a genuine mistake I made back there... about the creation and so forth. No offence given... or taken, I hope." I notice I am standing on a cloud. My feet are starting to slip through it at this point. I am thinking about Jesus walking on the water at Lake Galilee. Asking myself why I had to be so rational about things down below. Where on earth was my imagination?

"I shall go and check whether you are expected. If you would just be kind enough to wait for a..." He vanishes.

This is the part that does worry me. I suffer from vertigo at the best of times. Hate heights. Have not changed a light bulb since I was fifty. Mammy used to do all that. There she would be up the ladder. Her with the Parkinson's Disease and me feeling giddy just looking up. I would steady the ladder for her as best I could. Sure we were as good as a circus act, the two of us.

I wait on my cloud. No longer any sense of time passing. Waiting to know. When the man with the keys is with me I feel safe. I must hold out until he returns. Then, if I sink down into my cloud beyond my knees, I plan to save myself by launching myself onto his cloud. Grip his keys.

For the time being I occupy myself with a few extracts from Handel's Hallelujah Chorus. Sing as loudly as I can, "...And He shall reign for ever and ever... King of Kings... King of Kings and Lord of Lords... for ever... and ever... and ever... and ever." I secretly hope that somewhere He can hear me. The Keeper Of The Keys returns, his hands covering his ears, "Usually so peaceful on this gate..." he mumbles into his beard, then addresses me directly, "Saint Peter sends his regards. He remembers you back in Bagenalstown days but seems to have lost track of you since. Asked have there been any technical difficulties. Could your record be with the Romans or Greeks?"

"Certainly not. I can't understand it at all. His messages just do not seem to have got through to me for a while. Some sort of interference maybe. There were so many things to try to sort out... and, could it have been... experiments in the atmosphere... atomic bombs were exploded all through the decade before I died.. could that?..."

"Yes, yes. Exercise of Free Will. Very common. Worldly distractions. Run of the mill stuff for a Purgatory requirement. Saint Peter is a great believer in people being allowed to Make Choices... as is... You Know Who. 'He' is in a foul mood today too. 'She' is out doing good all over the world. If 'She' was here, She would tell me to slip you through. No problem. Sorry chum."

"I've had it then," I think to myself, and immediately a little cloud passes by. On it my thoughts openly displayed.

"Don't worry. He's not too bad. If you play it His way." The Keeper of The Keys has seen and heard it all before, "Know what I mean?"

"Well, it is His creation. It must be fascinating too, watching people groping their way along, struggling to reach the right road. He likes people to come to Him, does He? Does not believe in Mohammed having to go to the mountain..." I sense I have said the wrong thing. My companion looks distinctly

79

uneasy at the mention of the Holy Prophet's name. He confides sotto voce that there is a separate entrance further along for 'them'. It is the way it works best. No disrespect to other religions. The woman who looks after the Moslems' gate is quite a close friend. But you do different training courses for each of the various entrance gates. He has a pleading expression on his face, "We usually just stick to what we know. The Grand Committee thinks it works more smoothly that way. Everybody keeping together with their own kind..."

I am still on tenterhooks as Father Michael glides smoothly into view on a substantial looking cumulus powered by an energetic flock of angels. It hovers in the vicinity of The Keeper's cloud. Bagenalstown's erstwhile Parish Priest strides around with the sure-footed confidence of someone still on terra firma. His cloud seems in a rush. It edges forward. Tries to nudge The Keeper's cloud to one side, ignoring all formalities.

"Just a few brief questions, Michael. Father, that is? Parish Priest, Bagenalstown?"

"The one."

"What is your view, Michael, on the necessity for religious belief on earth?" Michael looks uncertain whether to demand the usual prefix, 'Father', from this lowly minion or not. Seems to conclude it would be disrespectful to The Father Of All to retain a title equivalent to His. To me The Keeper whispers, "A possible canonisation in the offing here. 'He' will probably put the idea in the Holy Father's mind some time over the next few centuries, when people have forgotten what Michael was like. You cannot fault him for unswerving conformity though. Listen to him..."

"The necessity for religious belief..." Having gathered his thoughts, Father Michael speaks quickly, all the while peering intently past The Keeper, to glimpse the inner sanctum beyond. "...is incontrovertible. Belief gives human nature, the most deeply flawed nature in the whole animal kingdom, the opportunity to rise above itself. Religious belief is the bedrock of Faith. It ensures salvation through Faith in God, the Creator of the universe."

"Could even be an Instant Entrant if he continues as well as this. Almost word perfect isn't he?" The Keeper nudges me as three puffs of cloud billow out from the inner sanctum. His eyes are sparkling with excitement. "If he gets three puffs after my next question as well, he is in. He'll be my first 'Instant' since Saint Thomas Aquinas came through here centuries ago."

Father Michael has not yet finished discoursing on the benefits of religious belief, "Firm belief in something without hard proof is Faith worth having – that is 'True Faith'. True Faith is a gift which comes directly from God. Those ignoramuses who reject belief in Him do not receive Faith. The 'doubting Thomases' of this worl... down on earth..." For the first time Father Michael looks uncertainly over the edge of his cloud, "...have only themselves to blame. No wonder they fail to find True Faith. They have closed minds. They will never enter God's Kingdom." Father Michael flinches as a Russian Orthodox priest, in tall black headwear and flowing robes, shoots past him like a rocket. "I am at the right gate, I trust?" Father Michael is bewildered and horror-struck by the possibility that undeserving non-Catholics have infiltrated the outer realms of his Eternal Heavenly Reward.

"Fear not, Michael. The just and righteous enter here. The Orthos have their own gate on the far side. Just a small one."

The Keeper speaks in a soothing tone. Guides Father Michael from his unruly cloud onto his own.

"One final question. Can you think of reasons why guidance and rules continue to be necessary on earth? A short answer will do..."

"Without rules they'd be out thieving, fornicating, giving way to slothfulness, seeking pleasure, getting up to no good. They are their own worst enemy. Half of them will not even give God one hour a week... they ignore His command to worship at weekly Mass. Think once a year is enough. Drunk at the Christmas Midnight Mass. Lolling about at the back. Going out to smoke during my sermon. Always just the faithful few who attend as they should. Participate in Parish activities. The others need a kick up their... discipline gives them all help to live happy and holy lives. A bit of fear does no harm. It is for their own good. Fear of the flames below and knowledge that virtue will be rewarded. That put most of us on the right road as children. Helped us to live at ease with our consciences..."

The Keeper spots three further emissions of cloud billowing from the inner sanctum, "Enter, friend." He gives Father Michael a toothless grin, "You Know Who will be down for the Induction Address... sometime. There are a few million others in... Just go in and relax... and thank you. Thank you for your life's work."

Father Michael transfers to a conveyor cloud which carries him automatically to the halo dispenser and beyond into the fluorescent brightness of the inner sanctum. I feel my cloud drift up and away, a gas-filled balloon torn by a capricious breeze from a child's hands.

Sean's words penetrate my mid-afternoon drowsiness, "Grandad... Are you awake? See my picture... a dolphin... a lovely dolphin, painted all the colours of the rainbow... It's looking for God under the sea..."

I am floating, gliding, darting, alongside the rainbow-coloured dolphin. Through raging Atlantic breakers, over waterfalls, tidal waves, through drifting mists, waterspouts, restful ripples, freezing seas, temperate oceans. If any spirit or essence remains of me when I depart this life, let it mingle with the waters of the earth. The opalescent streams of the River Barrow, the stillness of McDonagh's pond, the Bristol Channel's estuarial ebb and flow, Clarence Park's ornamental springs and fountains. Water to water. Not dust to dust.

"I'm going now, Grandad. Mummy and Daddy are back."

"Waaah... Phlppph..." I want to rest. I sleep a lot these days.

"Shall I put the blinds down and draw the curtains to help you to sleep, Grandad?"

"Ahhmm... mmm."

I do not want to wake. A familiar figure is approaching. Broad-shouldered. I know that stride. I call out, "Declan, hey Declan. Over here."

Declan motions that I should be silent. I notice there is blood streaming from my left leg, below the knee. Shattered bone pokes through the torn trouser leg. I feel no pain but blood is gushing out fast.

"Lie still. Just lie still and keep down. They will be looking for you. They want to meet you."

"Who does?"

"No names, closest brother. Names are not necessary."

Declan snaps the brown scapula which Dominic gave me from around my neck. Uses it as a tourniquet on my left thigh. I am lying in a grove, surrounded by tall trees. It is so familiar.

"Come nightfall we will get you to the farmhouse. No use in the daylight. They are everywhere. Can you hang on?"

I go to speak. No words. As if paralysed. The sun is sinking in the west. A rosy glow. I shiver. I will be in the farmhouse by dawn. Metallic rattling in the distance does not trouble the stillness of the trees. Rat, tat, tat. Once. Again. Declan crouches beside me, "Small arms fire. Just pot shots. No need to worry. They will not find us here." His words are confident, his brow furrowed. My head rests in Mary's lap. She is curving over so that her face is upside down above me. She massages my temples with what smells like lavender oil.

"You have been in the wars and no mistake, Mr Connolly."

"M...," There is so much I want to ask her. She places her hands along each side of my head.

"Sshhh. Don't talk. Just in case. There's not many have foreign accents in these parts."

I look into Mary's face. She has not changed. Not one grey hair. The same smooth, competent hands. My body lies spread-eagled, spent. The left leg at a crazy angle.

"We'll be needing a stretcher," Declan looks solemnly in Mary's direction.

"...And some will have to be told he is here. People we trust. It can't be avoided. He needs a doctor. It's life or death for him now," Mary strokes my cheeks. Kisses my forehead. Consoles me. As she would a horse with a broken fetlock. While waiting for the vet to arrive. To destroy it.

"It is not going to be easy," says Declan, as he gathers loose timbers to make poles for the stretcher.

"Sure, they may not recognise him... His appearance is quite different from when he left us," Mary seems to be mourning the passing of time. There is a faraway look in her eyes.

I try to lift one of my arms. To point. To draw their attention to the British Army uniform I am wearing. They must know it is suicide to be found wearing it. Yet they are acting quite normally. Making no effort to conceal it for me. Why? I feel weak. Drained. Everything grows dim.

"I think we may be losing him, Declan. He's slipping away from us..."

Mary's words are the last thing I hear as I open my eyes. My room is full of moving shadows. The curtains and blinds next to an open window are swaying to and fro. Two people stand in the corner. Staring straight ahead. To the right of the bay window. They advance slowly. Through the stripes of light thrown across the room by the venetian blinds, "Eh, Wah. Who is it? Who are you?" They do not answer. "Just tell me what you want? I've done nothing wrong."

They are leather clad. Black coats. Black masks. Black boots. I struggle up off the sofa. If they will not speak, I cannot help them. I move towards the window. Pass in front of the first figure. Feel his breath on my cheek. Sense fear. Shapes, brown, grey, black, merge, dapple, disengage, across the walls, the ceiling. Fleeting images of dogs, old mens' faces, birds of prey with wide, jagged-edged wings. I pull a cord. Raise one venetian blind. Another. And another. Sunlight streams in. No intruders. Outside, the cedars wave gently to me. The light is dazzling. I inch back to the sofa. Stare at the electric fire's red-glowing rods. Mesmerised. The concave shield behind the rods reflects heat. Throws it forward. Distributes it far and wide. Cold sweat slides down my flanks. Get up for my dressing gown. The one with tassels and braid enough to adorn a dress uniform. Golden tassels each end of the cord. Ruby braid edging around the hem. Braid loops on the sleeves. I get into my pyjama trousers. Squeeze into the corner of the sofa. Put my left hand tight up under my right armpit. My right tight under my left armpit. That will warm my hands. I will sit here quietly. Noreen will bring me tea later. I know she will.

"Pop. Awake yet?"

"Come in, Noreen. It's so good to see yous."

"Our guests have arrived. Remember... the dinner party? You agreed to come to this one. You will join us won't you?" Noreen has the air of a woman in the middle of doing a dozen things at once. I am still full from the delicious lunch. I need a wash. Will have to dress again. Noreen mentioned the dinner party to me days ago. I have forgotten it. Do not really want to make the effort. They are being so thoughtful, Noreen and Cecil. Introducing me to their friends. Making me feel welcomed in their home.

"We are going to eat in about five minutes," Noreen persists, but absently. I would not hurt their feelings for the world.

Noreen has already gone to the trouble of briefing me about the guests. Damien and Bernadette Lovelace are their closest friends. Both solicitors in private practice. They have six lovely children and holidayed with Noreen, Cecil and Sean in the Lake District last summer. Professor Don McNamara and his wife Moira have recently moved to Cardiff from Dublin. He was at Trinity College and has come across to take up the chair in Theology at the University of Wales, Cardiff. Moira is a social worker. Works with the deaf. They have bought themselves a house in Kings Road. In the same parish as Noreen and Cecil. Yvette John is a painter. Teaches at the art college. Met Noreen at some English Literature evening classes. Yvette wants Cecil to sit for a portrait but he keeps saying he has not got the time.

On special occasions, Noreen and Cecil use the middle room. The room has large French windows which give onto a back yard dominated by a castor oil tree. There are no other windows. Cecil draws the long velour drapes for dinner parties creating an atmosphere of intimacy. The table is decked out as grandly as a table for a Regimental Dinner in the Officer's Mess. All shining silver and cut glass. I often served at table in the Mess when they were short. This evening, at Cecil's and

Noreen's, I am treated as a guest of honour. It is grand.

"This is Pop, everyone." Noreen directs me to the chair nearest the door. She knows my prostate means I have to pay a visit sometimes during a meal.

I bow to each of the gentlemen in turn and kiss the ladies' hands. Moira and Yvette pull their hands away rather quickly, but Bernadette smiles warmly, mouths 'How charming'.

Silence descends, as it so often does as people start to eat. The soup is a consommé. I blow on each spoonful, discreetly, before it goes in. Do not want to be left behind. Everybody staring at me as I hurry to finish. Noreen hands me a piece of that French bread with the hard crust. I have to chew hard to get into it at all. A little soup helps to soften it. I still make a noise like a castanet clicking away with no musical accompaniment.

During the clearing away of the soup dishes, Cecil charges our glasses with chilled, white-green Frascati. It has a fresh, nutty flavour, with an unusual, attractive tang of slightly sour cream. So Noreen tells us. I would not have noticed. Still it goes down very nicely. Noreen's best wine glasses are enormous. Cecil fills them full. Never does things by halves. He would not want to offer their guests less than generous hospitality in any case.

The atmosphere gradually relaxes and I make short work of the coq au vin while the old friends get to know the newcomers. Every time the level in my glass goes down, Cecil is on his feet filling it up again. Yvette John likes a drop too. I can see that. She takes great gulps from her glass when she sees the level in mine is down. Knows Cecil will be around. And why not, I say? More power to her elbow. I have never had my portrait painted. It might be nice for the family to have such a thing, I think. For when I am gone.

The volume of conversation gets louder and louder... "Oh, I couldn't agree more... Quite so... Omnipotent Deity... All over my dress... Ha, ha, ha... Very much... Pax Romana... reactionary vestiges... Really?.. rampant episcopalianism... No!... going up to Oxford next term... Affairs, Diocesan first and foremost... Next to Marks and Spencers... a fortnight in Keswick, Keswick Manor... Samuel Beckett... waiting for the bus in Queen Street... so Pinteresque... the freshest greenest sprouts anywhere..."

"How would you like to do me?" I lean to my right side where Yvette sits.

"Paint you, Mr Connolly?" Yvette looks interested.

"It would be something for the family to remember me by... when I am gone, Miss John."

"Please, do call me Yvette. What a lovely thought. Noreen and Cecil would love that. A portrait can capture so much more of a person's character than a photograph. Mine do anyway." Yvette chuckles as she says this. Pats me on my thigh.

I can see it in my mind's eye. Me sitting nobly on a throne-like chair wrapped in ermine robes. Yvette gently angling my chin to just where she wants it. Then from behind her easel her observant, grey eyes scrutinising every inch of me. Drinking me in. Reading me. My life. My joys, my sorrows recorded in my time-worn features. It will be fun. I can see Yvette has a sense of humour. Sure why not go the whole hog? Our bodies carry us through life, not just our faces. I playfully grasp Yvette's wrist just as she is about to fork the last of her coq au vin in. "Yvette, there's nothing more I would like than to have me picture painted by you. But there's just one problem. I haven't a pouch. Y'wouldn't have one to lend me, would yous?"

Yvette lowers her fork, looks at me as if she is not sure she has heard correctly, "Do you mean a posing pouch, Mr Connolly?"

I do not notice the assembled company quietening, looking at us, their attention probably attracted by my movement in grasping Yvette's wrist.

"A posing pouch. That's what they're called is it? Or should I dispense with a posing pouch altogether. Eh, wha'? What say you, Yvette?" I notice a bright red flush is spreading up Yvette's neck and she is studying her wine glass with great intensity. A sea of faces is turned towards me. Eyes fix me with a disapproving gaze. I am condemned, adjudged to have sinned. I feel it behoves me to somehow salvage the moment. I lean forward to pass around the bread basket, "Please... take... eat." The un-accustomed act of stretching in every direction causes my truss to creak more loudly than usual. The guests are distracted. Look in the direction of the door thinking it is in need of oiling.

"No, no. That noise was me truss," I explain. Cecil's and

Noreen's eyes are wide open. And their mouths. I would not have thought they were that interested in the old truss. Still the others look interested as well. Apart from Yvette. Her shoulders are shaking. As if she is choking on a fish bone. That is not possible. It was chicken we ate. If I was not sure she was incapable of unkindness, I would think she was stifling laughter.

"It happened at The Front. That was in the Great War of course. Signals was my job. Had to shift a heavy coil of copper cable... Try saying that after a few glasses of Frascati, Yvette, eh, wha'..." Noreen looks as if she wants to remind me of something I have left out but I remember it all perfectly well, "Shifted this cable in a bit of a hurry one day. 'Pop' went Pop... good one that, eh, Noreen? That was the war more or less over for me. Got more and more difficult after that. Affected me nerves. Just a young man, you see. Thought a corner of a foreign field was going to be forever Bagenalstown as it were. Where I was born, you see, Bagenalstown. Don't expect yous realised I was born an Irishman?"

Damien ignores my question, "'Dulce et decorum est pro patria mori'. As the old lie goes." An erudite fellow. No doubt about it.

"What are your views on pacifism, Damien?" Noreen swiftly follows up.

I have not finished yet. I can see the others are still interested, it would be rude not to complete what I am saying.

"Hernia op in Blighty. Fixed it for a few years. Didn't last. Fitted up really well now though. Look at that for workmanship." I manage to squeeze the top of the lovely calf leather harness through the front buttons of my shirt.

"Thank you, Pop." Noreen looks at me the way she looks at Sean sometimes. I do not want to monopolise the conversation. If truth be told I could not eat another thing. I rise to my feet, "Ladies and gentlemen, honoured guests of Noreen and Cecil. It is a custom in Ireland... you'll know this Don and Moira... to end your meal with a song. To show your appreciation to the host and hostess. So will I give you a song before I go?"

"Oh, please do." Bernadette is one of those kind people who cannot resist responding, saying the right thing.

I tuck my chin in. Hold my right arm before my chest, my

hand half open in a gesture of giving. Take a deep breath. In advance, imagine their appreciative response, "What a truly mellifluous voice you have, Mr Connolly," Bernadette is sure to say. Or something like it. "Bully for you, sir," Damien Lovelace will shout in the sort of voice people use when cheering runners in a race. The rest will clap and bang the table and demand more. I can hear them. I stretch as tall as I can, ignoring loud cracking and creaking sounds from my truss, agonised wrenching sounds like a tree about to topple...

OH DANNY BOY, THE PIPES,
THE PIPES ARE CALLING,
FROM GLEN TO GLEN AND
ROUND THE MOUNTAINSIDE.
THE SUMMER'S GONE AND
WINTER'S IN THE MEADOW.
IT'S YOU, IT'S YOU MUST GO
AND I MUST BIDE...

"Splendid, Pop." Noreen cuts me off in mid-note, loudly and firmly. I must let them get on with their party. She skilfully guides the conversation forward, "Pop's song reminds me we are going over to visit Ireland in the school holidays. Pop's brother and family in Bagenalstown..."

"Ah... Muine Bheag... a lovely part," Professor McNamara looks speculatively at me as if expecting some response.

"Well, goodnight to all of yous. Thank you kindly for the pleasure of your company."

In silence I take the few steps necessary to reach the door. "I think I may have a touch of that old biliousness coming on me again, Noreen..."

"Andrews Liver Salts are in the bathroom, Pop. Take three or four spoons of that."

"I will, Noreen. Bless you. I will. Bless all of you..."

"Sleep well, Mr Connolly," Bernadette pipes up in her kindly way.

"Remember. You're walking to Mass with Sean tomorrow morning..." Noreen is carrying the cream covered gateaux across from the sideboard.

"I was just thinking, Noreen..."

"Good night, Pop."

Upstairs I get into my pyjama trousers. Never have bothered with pyjama jackets. The seams get twisted. Cut off the blood. Make my arms go numb.

I breathe deeply before getting into bed. Tonight I feel fuddled. That Frascati was wine in a million. I expand my chest. Fine ribs I have. An impressive specimen of nine stone manhood, even if I say so myself. Some small modifications needed. Just a few. I drum on my sides like a prize-fighter. That portrait would have been something. I would like to have seen Yvette in action. I love a woman with a sense of humour. She would have enjoyed painting me I am sure. Pity. I do not think she is going to follow up our arrangement now. I just got that impression.

I sip the Andrews Liver Salts. What a kick. The bubbles go straight up my nose. As good as smelling salts any day. Happily the biliousness is passing off. I pummel my chest again to celebrate victory over physical indisposition. Cough uncontrollably. But only for a moment. Thump the chest once more. Check robustness. Ah. Much better. Seems to be a bit of draught coming under the door though.

Into bed. Fresh sheets. Noreen gets them so clean. Perfumed. Starched as stiff as new all week. It is like sleeping between fragrant sheets of ice. The washing machine has been a godsend. Automatic. Thick blankets are tucked tightly in place on each side of the mattress. Anchor things in place nicely. I feel so secure. Hardly move all night sometimes.

I will sleep soon. At day's end I turn my thoughts to Mammy. Say goodnight at the window before getting into bed. Forgot tonight. Sit up. Feet out again. Slowly across the room in the dusk. Push aside curtain, venetian blind. Gaze in the direction of Ely cemetery. The sky is clear. Stars out. Left my spectacles on the bedside table. Cannot see the star which I believe looks after Mammy at night-time. Just a blue haze. She will understand. I was always forgetting things. I blow her a kiss. My reflection in the window pane does the same. Mammy will see me wishing her goodnight wherever she is. I hope it helps her.

In the road, I notice a man leaning against the lamppost opposite our house. A touch of the biliousness comes on me again. He is big built. Like our friend, Dermot, from the Saint Vincent de Paul Society. Smoke rings hover in the air above him. No buses pass this way. He is watching us. I hurry back to bed.

I try to dwell on happy thoughts. They escape me. I recall that Dermot has not been back to see me for months. But I am still on his list. The church bus now calls every Sunday to take me to Mass. Noreen makes excuses for me but the drivers are beginning to get impatient with her. That is why I am walking to Mass in the morning with Sean. To prove that I can do it. To get myself off their list. Sean and I can slip quietly into a bench at the back of church just as the Mass starts. Inconspicuous. Then away again after the priest's communion, a few minutes before the Mass ends. They say Dermot is still back and fore in this area. If I travelled down in Cecil's car he would be sure to spot us. There he would be in a flash. Bending down. Making conversation at the passenger window. Even before Cecil would have a chance to apply the brake. He would be wanting to visit the family in Ireland. Getting details. Addresses. Digging into our history. I feel myself drifting off. Awaken again with a start. Felt I was falling. Fell with a bump. My body is warm. My feet are stone cold. I will sleep now. Rest my feet for the walk to Mass in the morning.

The milkman's cart slides and scrapes down Marlborough Hill. Horse hooves slither desperately on the gravel. The roundsman goes into a paroxysm of anger, as if the horse itself has caused a hill to be in this place. "Whoaaa... Betsy. WHOAAA." The harness rattles. Bottles chime in wire crates. Reins are being pulled tight in. The blankets covering my head do nothing to keep the noise out. It is Sunday morning. My stomach churns as I recall the morning's plans. The desirability of changing the arrangement occurs to me as Noreen's reassuring tread and the tinkle of teaspoon on china fall like music on my ears.

"I was just thinking..."

"Again, Pop?"

"I think me varicose veins are worse again..."

"Walking to church will do them good. Here... try not to be too long with your breakfast."

Noreen places a tray bearing my bowl of prunes, a nice green apple and a hot cup of tea, on the bedside table. In health matters Noreen has an unerring instinct. She is right. If you stop and think about it, walking will probably do my circulation no end of good.

"Sean is all ready and waiting downstairs in his Sunday best," Noreen says firmly.

"Tell him, 'Up and at 'em. Grandad will be there before you can say Jack Robinson'."

Noreen has a straightness to her back as she leaves the room. She is so proud of Sean. So she should be. He is as good as gold.

One of my shoelaces snaps as I strain to tie my shoes securely for the long walk ahead. There seem to be so many small tasks to do. Unavoidable routines. It is frustrating at times like this. I cannot deny it. Everything seems to take longer and longer. In my wooden box on the mantelpiece I search for a spare lace. String, elastic bands, paper clips, drawing pins, collar studs, sealing wax, styptic pencils, pieces of chalk, Beech Nut chewing gum for Sean, buttons, pens. All sorts of things are in there. Not always what I want. This morning I am in luck. One brown lace. No black ones. It will have to do. Threading it through the eyelets in my shoe is an exacting business. Shoes on. Just time to wolf breakfast down. I dislike the taste of prunes but my bowels have been on strike for the last three days. I hope eating plenty of fruit will do the trick.

Sean and I step out in brisk military fashion. He, in a new, blue bow tie, white shirt, grey shorts and brogues. I, in cream jacket, white flannels, polished black boots – one black, one brown lace, and the old bottle-green trilby on top.

"You look the cat's whiskers today, Sean," I say patting him on his head.

"You too, Grandad... except for your shoelaces." Sean does not have a dishonest bone in his body.

We are up Victoria Avenue in no time. Mrs O'Brien's curtains are still drawn. Through Clarence Park, past the flowerbeds and statue, in no time at all. Along Daisy Road I shorten my stride. The apple and prunes are beginning to have an effect. By the time we reach Saint Oswald's Hospital, lower down Daisy Road, I can walk no further. There are two driveways. Entrance and Exit. High brick walls flank the points where they join Daisy Road. I press my back against the Exit wall, clenching my buttocks together hard.

"Grandad needs the toilet, Sean." I look helplessly in the direction of the hospital.

Several nursing nuns, in pristine white habits, are looking out, placing vases of flowers on window sills in the wards. They think I am a charming old man admiring the flourishing rosebeds in the hospital grounds. They wave at me. Such a friendly gesture. One I would normally return without a moment's hesitation. I dare not wave back. I press my back even harder against the wall. It will look odd if I do not acknowledge them. I risk a quick nod. A fleeting grin. The concentrated muscle tension in my buttocks is momentarily unsettled. I recover just in time. Mind over matter alright. If only I could get to one of the nun's bedpans I would be the happiest man in Cardiff. The distance up the driveway is too great. Could never make it. Would be ready to feed the rosebeds before I was thirty yards along. The nuns would not be so happy with me then.

"See them... ah!... houses across the road, Sean?" I have never seen the little man look so worried.

"Yes, Grandad."

"Knock and ask if your grandad can use their... ah!... toilet. There's a good boy. Quick..."

What I have often wished for in other circumstances, happens. Time stands still. I am in a trance as Sean sprints across the road. Each footfall takes an eternity. He is no longer wearing smart brown brogues but divers' weighted boots.

While Sean heads for the first house, a rusty, blue van, full of elderly folk, turns into the driveway marked 'Entrance'. The urgency in my bowels increases. Dermot is driving. He does not see me. Concentrates on wrenching the steering wheel around to guide the van into the entrance. I spot Mrs O'Brien squashed into a rear seat. On her head a black lace mantilla covers her beautiful copper curls. I must get away before Dermot collects his passenger and passes through this exit. We all have our exits and our entrances and one man in his time plays many parts. My final exit may not be far off if Dermot finds me.

At the first house, Sean is speaking politely to a ginger-haired man. The man is wearing a vest. Looks puffy around the eyes. I guess Sean's knock on the door has woken him up. I try to catch his eye. To let him know I am just a silly old man in a predicament. Apologetic. Will not stay long. Will be no trouble. The words, "...bloody nuisance...", drift across the road. I see the door closing. Sean moves on to the next house. He waves at me to reassure me he is doing his best. I try to respond without moving too much. All that happens is that my cheeks tremble and I squeek, "Yip", like a frightened field mouse.

One moment, the urgent promptings of my bowels are intense. The next, they subside. But they never go away. Angry at my lack of moral fibre, I seek supernatural intercession. I have often found Litanies' worth a try in a tight spot. I resort to the Litany of The Saints. That one has never failed me.

From Thy wrath	Deliver us, O Lord
From sudden and unprovided death	Deliver us, O Lord
From the snares of the devil	Deliver us, O Lord

From anger, hatred and ill will	Deliver us, O Lord
From the spirit of fornication	Deliver us, O Lord
From lightning and tempest	Deliver us, O Lord
From sickness and diarrhoea	Deliver us, O Lord
From the scourge of earthquake	Deliver us, O Lord.

It is a minor miracle. I am able to hang on.

In the second house, only a madly barking dog is at home. The spirit moves again within me. I cannot wait much longer. On the doorstep of the third house, a tall man, in white turban and bus conductor's uniform, listens carefully to what Sean is saying. Sean points across the road at me. My mouth gapes in a rictus of agonised restraint. From a distance it probably looks like a smile. The man gestures that I am welcome to enter his house.

I lie on my bed. Two tablespoons of kaolin and morphine have soothed my insides. I am glad to have a good reason to come home. Having let everything go, I feel so much better. Noreen says I hold things in too much. Then get over-excited. I have been worked up about the trip to Ireland. It is true. Looking forward to it. Worrying too. That Dermot fellow. Interfering all the time. It is hard enough preparing yourself to go back. Not knowing who you will meet altogether. Wondering how you will be received. I am not the man who left. They will be meeting a stranger. A stranger's family. If Declan is married to Mary McDonagh, it will be a strange reunion too. For all of us. Enough. Noreen is right. I do think about things too deeply. There is nothing to be done. Only to travel in hope. Strange. Since Declan's letter I have been thinking more about Mammy. As a young woman. Our life together. As if I do not want to go travelling. Leaving her here. Alone.

I am behind the counter of the Post Office in Market Drayton. My eye is distracted by a cluster of brightly coloured hats sitting prettily on a group of young women who have taken shelter from an April shower, beneath the arches outside the Post Office doors.

As I go out at lunchtime, they are still there. "Are you visitors to the town?" I ask. "Can I assist you in any way at all?" I have not been out of the army long. Still penniless. In lodgings. Have affected the manners of a dandy. Without the resources or position to remotely justify doing so. Expecting a swift rebuff, I add, "If you would care to join me, ladies, I am about to take lunch at The Crown in Queen Street. Maybe you would find there an antidote to this inclement weather."

"How kind of you." A woman standing at the back of the group speaks up in the gentlest voice I have ever heard. "We would love to..." People at this time usually look suspiciously at me when I speak. Comment on there being something unusual about my accent. Suggest that I cannot be from these parts. Ask where the name, Connolly, comes from anyway. Step back when told it is an Irish name.

In The Crown, Florence sits next to me. It is she who has the gentle voice. She explains she and her friends have travelled over from Chester via Nantwich by train. Just for the day. A dressmakers' day out. Her eyes are a baby blue colour. They never changed. I demonstrate for her and her friends the local custom of dipping fresh gingerbread into a glass of port. Consuming both. Then repeating the process. It makes for a fine lunch on a wet April afternoon. We all laugh a lot. Florence is dressed in a shaped blue skirt, full cut jacket with wide lapels and rucked upper sleeves. A cream blouse. A velvet choker displaying a delicate cameo brooch. Looks every inch a lady. So poised. She explains she makes all her own clothes.

Florence and I find it easy talking to each other. She lives beside Chester's River Dee. Her parents own a small hotel. She bites deep into a piece of gingerbread. Small crumbs balance on her upper lip. Her mouth, slightly trembling, above the rim of her glass, is poised to drink. A small amount only. Port washes the crumbs away.

I have to return to work. The rain has stopped. My companions decide to leave too. I politely step back to let Florence's friends pass. I follow Florence. As she steps before me, I cannot help looking down. To admire her trim waist. Trim ankles. The graceful line of her neck sweeping up to the plaits of thick brown hair tucked beneath her hat. The firmness of her breasts, apparent even beneath the full cut jacket and viewed from a position behind Florence's shoulder. As I lift my eyes I notice a mirror hanging on the oak-panelled wall. 'Players Please' in red letters at the top. Beneath the letters, Florence's innocent blue eyes. She has been watching in the mirror as I admired her appearance. The expression on her face is undisturbed, well-mannered, enigmatic. Out of the bar. The women slowly flow. Talking of where next to go.

We come to a halt outside the Post Office. "Should you be in these parts again, please remember, I am at your service, ladies." My heart is sinking. In seconds they will be strolling off. To look around the town. Later to board a steam train for Chester. I may never meet this kind, lovable woman again. I stand transfixed.

"Goodbye... goodbye." They are already drifting off down the street. Florence lingers for a few extra seconds. Perhaps sensing my turmoil.

"I wonder... Would you do me the honour of taking tea with me this Saturday afternoon?"

"Why... yes."

"Four o'clock, then. Outside The Crown?"

Florence smiles. Shakes my hand. Is gone.

Saturdays become days when every second is experienced so intensely an hour could be passing. Yet hours pass like seconds. At my lodgings Mrs Crutchley brews us tea in her china pot with the hen's nest tea cosy. We relish her delicious damson cake without really tasting it. Have to resist her generous hospitality. Her entreaties to have ..."just one more slice". With the selfish instinct of youth, Mammy and I are only really aware of each other's presence during tea. I think of Florence as Mammy even then, though I did not call her that until Cecil was born.

"She is a lovely lass, that." Mrs Crutchley takes a special interest in our progress, in the absence of other parental figures in Market Drayton. "You want to look after her, Mr Connolly. You could lose her so easily you know." She always sends Mammy off laden with numerous napkins bursting with sandwiches, damson cake, gingerbread, scones.

It feels like being at a tea party in a doll's house at Mrs Crutchley's. Her cottage is a simple two up, two down, building. A coal fire in the parlour heats the oven. Both are tucked away beneath a small wooden mantelpiece. The oven's iron door is glazed with warm, red tiles. Its silver handle glitters like precious stones in the gaslight.

In Mammy's company, Market Drayton becomes an enchanted place. Walking with her past the tiny artisans' dwellings, the miniature manor houses, through the intricate web of streets, alleys and footpaths, feels like walking through a whole town of dolls' houses, through a model town cut off from the harsher side of life. It is as if it is there just for us, for our pleasure and enjoyment. Whether strolling along the banks of the River Tern, resting on canvas chairs on the veranda of the cricket pavilion pretending to watch the cricket, or skirting the edge of swaying barley fields, watching the heads of the barley nodding at us as we pass acknowledging our joy at walking there together. It costs us nothing to rest in the peaceful churchyard of Saint Mary's, the Parish Church. We shed a tear for the lovers all around whose love is preserved there forever. We have all the time in the world. Over and over again, we are drawn to the watermill beneath the sandstone ridge upon which the town stands. The giant wheel turning in the stream's drift. Water rising. Falling. Through its giant spokes. Splashing with joy like a leaping trout as it falls back, blends once more with the full flow of the river.

We know few people well, apart from Mrs Crutchley. Those whose lives touch ours sense in us something apart, sacrosanct. At least that is how it feels to me at the time. Putting my arm around Mammy's shoulders, feeling her thigh against mine as we stroll along, noticing an involuntary judder of excitement run through her as we embrace; pleasure seems to bind us, into a relationship so full that we need nothing else. Through each week, a sense of Mammy's liveness plays in my thoughts; lifting her down from a stile, the touch of her fingers on the nape of my neck; until I can be with her again the next Saturday.

By July it is time to visit Mammy's family in Chester. Her parents invite me to Sunday dinner. They do me proud. I meet all Mammy's brothers and sisters. Her brother, Tommy, I learn, is a survivor of The Great War, like myself. A quiet, restrained man. We get on like a house on fire. I ask him to be my best man at our wedding. He willingly agrees.

Tommy gently insists he must take me for a stag night a week before the wedding. Just him and me. Old soldiers together. He takes me to The Boathouse beside the River Dee. It is a lovely spot. Sunset. A broad expanse of open water. Happy young people inside. Straw boaters. Striped blazers. Rowing club badges. Filigree designs. Crossed oars. Rowing boats. Women in flowing chiffon. Flowers in their hair. Effervescent. Laughing. Flirting. Living for the moment.

Tommy guides me to a table in a quiet corner. In the Cheshire Regiment he fought. Still only twenty. Looks forty. Had a hard time of it. Invalided out. We talk of Mammy and the rest of the family. His eyes light up, then soften, "They have been wonderful. Mean everything to me."

It is a hot evening. My last as a 'free' man, as Tommy jokes. We drink four or five pints of beer. He is a kindly best man. Talks of Mammy with such affection, "She is a peach. The best girl in the world. You are going to be very happy together. I can tell..."

As the evening wears on, the noise in the rest of the bar increases. People are in high spirits. I notice Tommy is acting rather strangely. He seems unable to disregard the presence of the people around. He begins to make a low, growling sound in the back of his throat. Picks up a beer mat. Gnaws on it. Spits pieces of it everywhere. Does not seem to hear me asking if he is alright. Suddenly he is on the floor. Crawling forwards using his elbows. Around the legs of the surprised customers standing in the bar. Some think he is just involved in high jinks of some sort. They laugh at him. Tommy springs to his feet. Aims imaginary blows at non-existent people. Keeps ducking his head. Flinching. Wide-eyed. Terrified. Finally he lets me approach him. I talk to him quietly. "It will be all right, Tommy. We will go home now. Shall we do that? See Florence... and your mother?" A little more relaxed, he allows me to guide him out of The Boathouse. He still holds one arm aloft, defending himself, as if there is an enemy force lurking in The Boathouse. He keeps muttering, "They don't know. None of them know. But the day will come. The day will come. Sooner than any of us knows..." He keeps his eyes fixed on The Boathouse until we are safely around the corner, out of sight. Mammy told me later

Tommy did not normally get as upset as that. It must have been the alcohol that triggered it off.

During the weeks before our wedding, I travel to Chester every week. We spend much time beside, in and on the river. Mammy is a great oarswoman. No sooner does the boathand shove us out than she has us skimming across the surface with deft flicks of the oars. Never a hatpin, bow or buckle out of place, however far we travel. One day we picnic far upstream. Surrounded by countryside. After eating we lie on a blanket. Listen to the honey bees and flies buzzing in the summer heat.

"I will love y'forever," I shout so it echoes in all directions and terrifies some ducks paddling quietly by.

"I will always love you, too." Mammy says it in a very loud voice for her. Has difficulty saying it at all, she is laughing so much.

We had often said we loved one another before. This was the most important time.

Before our wedding. Meaning it. The river our witness.

I could eat like a horse in those days. Never had to worry about my digestion. I am at least comfortable here on the bed. But I keep listening to my stomach rumbling. Thinking about it. I take another spoonful of kaolin and morphine just in case. My hands smell of Wright's Coal Tar Soap as I spoon it in. The medicine dries on my lips, leaving them caked and white. I picture myself looking like one of them stone figures on the tombs in Llandaff Cathedral. I join my hands on my chest. I feel the part. But stone statues do not have rumbling stomachs. Thanks be then for a rumbling stomach. Better to have one than not. It is so. And one should look after it. Soothing food and drink are essential. Like ginger beer. Noreen packed bottles of it in when we went down to the Llandaff Regatta a few weeks ago.

The sun is burning down. Noreen spreads a white tablecloth over the picnic table. We make short work of chicken legs and several bottles of ginger beer. No biliousness at all afterwards. Much better than hiding away in the old beer tent and missing all the rowing races.

Noreen turns her face to the sun, "I do love it here, Cecil."

"Excellent vista." Cecil has brought his binoculars.

Noreen busies herself with collecting our empty bottles and chicken bones. Goes into the club house to find a litter bin.

I rest happy on my deck-chair, grease dribbling down my chin. Enjoying the view. The rowing club is among trees. A lawned area slopes to the River Taff. Sean has acquired a programme. Reads out the names of some of the competing clubs. He reads well. I fill in the counties the places are in. I do not know who is the worse show-off. Sorting letters in the Post Office taught me where every place name in Britain was located. I cannot forget them for the life of me.

"Bew-d-ley Rowing Club. Is that right, Grandad?"

"Spot on, Sean. In Worcestershire... where the sauce comes from."

"Ironbridge Rowing Club. That's an easy one."

"And it's in Shropshire... where the iron bridge is."

"Saint John's College, Oxford."

"That's Oxford in Oxford-shire."

Cecil pricks up his ears, "You could go there, son. When you are older. If you work hard."

"Would I like it there, Dad?"

Cecil is now looking up river where a cox'less pairs race has started between Saint John's Oxford and Hereford Cathedral School.

A row of ruddy-faced supporters, beer glasses in hand, lines up on the clubhouse verandah.

"Saint John's... Saint John's... Saint John's..." they chant. Sean joins in with them. He has found an empty beer glass lying about on the lawn. He waves it above his head like the others.

"Two, four, six, eight... Who do we appreciate..?" another group screams at the top of their voices, "...HEREFORD!"

"Hereford in Herefordshire," I murmur. It is a compulsive habit, "Where the bulls come from."

Saint John's have it by a nose.

"Three minutes. Twenty five. Point four." Cecil records something on his clipboard. He is a timekeeper. A committee member. Proud of the Llandaff Rowing Club. In their eleventh year now. Expanding every year.

"Half past three, the next race. Women's Senior Eights. Minerva Bath against Wallingford." Cecil waits as the teams get ready for the start. A crew of honey-blondes strides past, their boat balanced easily, at arm's length, above their heads.

"Time for a stroll to the marquee for a coffee," I say. My legs get stiff if I sit too long. Bath Minerva have their boat in. Are pulling hard upstream. Blades flashing in the sun. Long legs flexing in unison. 'Red Hot' – the name of their boat. They are in with a good chance. Wallingford are floundering. No rhythm. Cannot get under way. They are drifting down river. Dangerously near the weir. The race marshal's boat tows their bow around. Out of danger.

I pause outside the tent. Drink in the atmosphere. Crowds mingling. Watching the drama on the river. A lull before the race starts. Rowers gossiping in groups, reclining on the grass. Glancing at each other. Enjoying being admired. Oar blades in every colour of the rainbow. Flags. Pennants. Team vests. On the far bank tall green trees against a sparrow's egg sky. Royal blue the marquee behind me. Canvas walls decorated with purple castellated strips. A place of sanctuary. No-one is watching me. Inside. It is cool in here. Perhaps something to warm me up first of all. A familiar voice calls, "Mr Connolly... here." I just order coffee. It is Mrs O'Brien who has spotted me. She points to an empty chair at her table, "Do join us." Two attractive girls are with her. "These are my nieces, Anna and Liz, Mr Connolly. I have come to watch them compete in the regatta."

I doff my hat. "Which club, girls?"

"Llandaff R.C." Anna pronounces the two L's in Llandaff the Welsh way.

"I'm coxing in the next race." Liz looks excited.

"Then we're together in the final of the cox'less pairs," they say with one voice.

I sense Mrs O'Brien staring at me. The way people do when they know you are suffering from a serious illness.

"Off you go, girls. I'll be fine here with Mr Connolly." A copy of W.B. Yeats's poems lies open on the table in front of Mrs O'Brien.

"Yeats! My favourite poet."

"Really, Mr Connolly?"

"'Down by the salley gardens my love and I did meet;
She passed the salley gardens with little snow-white feet.
She bid me take love easy, as the leaves grow on the tree;
But I, being young and foolish, with her would not agree.
In a field by the river my love and I did stand,
And on my leaning shoulder she laid her snow-white hand.
She bid me take life easy, as the grass grows on the weirs;
But I was young and foolish, and now am full of tears.'"

I take a sip of coffee.

"Foolish. But not as young as I was. Certainly not as young as I was, Mrs O'Brien."

"Nonsense. And beautifully recited. With such feeling."

"You are very kind."

"'In a field by the river my love and I did stand...'" Mrs O'Brien repeats the words slowly. Meaningfully. Irish music is in her voice.

"Join us for tea this evening, Mrs O'Brien. Cecil and Noreen would love to see you. We will spend all evening reciting Yeats. Up in my room. I have several rare first editions."

"I'd love to. But I couldn't leave the dog so long."

"Some other time?"

"No... Tell you what, Mr Connolly. Come to me instead. It'll be quieter at my house. We'll not be disturbed."

Mrs O'Brien lives at the top of Victoria Avenue. Three minutes walk from Noreen and Cecil's. Two and a half today. My haste is ridiculous. I must look a fool. I reach her front gate, weak from exertion. Pause to admire the garden. A small patch overshadowed by the house. Red rose bushes, green garden gnomes, struggling for daylight.

"Welcome... Welcome." My hostess takes my walking stick and straw hat. Places them on the hall-stand. For a moment I am lost without them. Paddy, the golden retriever, swiftly distracts me. I follow Mrs O'Brien, marvelling at the colour of her hair in the darkened hallway – burnished gold. Paddy follows me. Two large paws begin groping around my hips. He seems to think I have been brought here to slake his insatiable lust. Pressing on me heavily from behind, Paddy prances forward on his hind legs. Like a circus dog. But determined to gain purchase. What breed he thinks I am I do not know. He seems beyond caring. Finds me irresistible. His last assault catapults me forwards in a uncontrolled rush. Hampered by the darkness, I tumble. Headlong down the two steps leading from the hallway to the breakfast room. I clutch hastily at the figure of Mrs O'Brien. Luckily her muscles are well toned. From walking the dog every day. All woman. She assists me to a fully standing position. We face each other.

"Forgive me... I am so sorry... Lost my balance...

'An aged man is but a paltry thing,

A tattered coat upon a stick...' eh, what, Mrs O'Brien?" I straighten my tie. Try to regain some dignity.

"Yeats, again, Mr Connolly? How about...

...'And yet the beauties that I loved

Are in my memory;

I spit into the face of Time

That has transfigured me.'"

"Well said, ma'am. You have matched me. A sentiment I endorse. Entirely."

"You're not transfigured, sir. Plenty more beauties to store in your memory I'll warrant."

She is so kind, so generous. Takes me by the hands. Leads me to the tea table. Brings in egg and cress sandwiches. Slices of madeira cake. Tea. Almond slices. Swiss roll. I notice a framed photograph of a handsome man on the sideboard, half hidden behind a vase of white carnations. At last Mrs O'Brien sits down beside me.

"'She carries in the dishes,
And lays them in a row.
To an isle in the water
With her would I go.'" I can hardly believe how well I am remembering these quotations from Yeats. And such apt ones too.

"Oh. No more of that old fool Yeats, now, Mr Connolly." Mrs O'Brien leans against me as she passes the egg and cress sandwiches. Her perfume is fresh. Delicate. More like eau de cologne than perfume. "You can get too much of him. Don't you think?"

"I do that, Mrs O'Brien."

"Tell me. How have you been keeping? It must be nearly six months since you lost your wife. Florence wasn't it? How have you been coping?"

"I miss her, Mrs O'Brien. I miss her so much..."

"Tell me all about it then..."

I surprise myself. It is so easy to talk to Mrs O'Brien. I weep. Rain after the long drought. She knows. Understands. Of course she understands. She has been through it. A fine man her husband was too, by the look of his picture. I tell Mrs O'Brien how brave Mammy was. How hard it was to watch her go, at the end. She talks a little about her husband, Michael. How close they had always been. How the pain never goes. Just gets a little easier.

She sees how moved, distressed, I am. Gets a bottle from the sideboard. Pours some Jameson's into my tea. Full to the brim. It is such a relief to talk about my feelings. To talk about the good

105

times Mammy and I shared. Not just the grief. The splendour of our life together. Memories of our wedding. How proud of Mammy I was that day. Mrs O'Brien is interested. Has never seen the inside of a Protestant church herself. Wants to hear about the wedding service.

Chester Cathedral. A fine setting for the ceremony. Mammy's dress shimmers and blazes like the insides of a thousand oyster shells. Satin and silk encasing a body as beautiful and unflawed as the most perfect pearl. Up the aisle, arm in arm with her father, as naturally and gracefully as if she is on one of our strolls around Market Drayton. She smiles at all her relatives and friends in the left hand aisle. She does not have to concern herself with the other aisle. Behind her brother, Tommy, and me, are rows and rows of empty benches. Just my landlady, Mrs Crutchley, in the bench immediately behind us. Mammy greets her warmly. Mrs Crutchley sits beaming. A job well done. Her warnings about how easily I could lose Mammy have been fully heeded. I never really thought for a moment that I would lose her. Mrs Crutchley forces a little package into my hand. Gingerbread for the journey later. I am eternally grateful to her.

I feel so happy. I sing the opening hymn at the top of my voice. Black dots flicker and dart before my eyes. I am going to faint. A vision of myself collapsing in front of all these people flashes before me. Why do I always feel faint in church? What a way to start a marriage. I ease back. Control my enthusiasm. Steady myself on the kneeler. Recover.

The vicar makes me feel welcome. Conducts the ceremony with simple dignity. I discover the service is not much different from the Catholic one. Strange what all the fuss is about. Some beautiful singing too. Clear soprano voices climbing. To the roof of the Cathedral. Into the air outside. Beautiful sound reaching far and wide. Across the whole of Chester. Celebrating our union. The rest of the day is a blur. Meeting so many new people. Making a speech for the first time in my life. I cannot wait to get away. Mammy's father gives me money. "Long life and happiness to you both. Look after her well." I shake his hand.

A massive wardrobe dominates our room in the guest house at Porthmadog. A large mirror covers the length of the wardrobe door. Our room is tiny. I see Mammy wherever I look. She rests in a pink lace negligee. Leafs through the wedding cards. We talk about the day. We lie back quietly. Side by side. Mammy is yielding in my arms. After a few minutes she sits up. Crosses her arms and pulls her garment up. Removes it completely. She gets off the bed and stands hesitantly beside the mirror.

"Come and stand here with me..." She beckons. Half urgently. Half shyly. I scramble out of my wedding suit. Clothes in a heap on the floor beside the bed. Move to Mammy in front of the mirror.

"...and your socks." She laughs gently at my incongruous appearance.

I tug the socks off. Flick them over my shoulder. We look at each other in the glass. Turn to face each other. Hold each other. The front of our bodies just touching. My hands move up and down Mammy's smooth back. We press close together. My arms go right around her. Press her softness firmly against my chest. Mammy moves her feet. Her legs are parted. Trembling. In the mirror I see our limbs and bodies entwined. One figure. A fleshed sculpture. Breathing. Swaying. I taste Mammy's mouth. It is hot. Sweet from the pieces of gingerbread we have been eating. The swelling whiteness of Mammy's skin, where it is pressed hard against my darker body, is like dawn light before the rising of the sun. I slide into her with the suddenness and smoothness of fruit falling to earth.

In the mornings we walk to Morfa Bychan, Black Rock Sands. Enjoy the openness of the place. Its timelessness. Its remoteness. Neither of us is ready yet to share the other with the normality of daily life. We swim naked. A mile out. Our bodies stinging in the salt water. Mammy rests her hands on my shoulders. Lies back. Floating. I paddle forwards slowly. Kiss her upturned belly. Watch her thick brown hair coil itself around her floating breasts. We linger in the embrace of the sea until we are cold. Then head back to the town.

"Oh, yes. A superb wedding, Mrs O'Brien. A lovely service. I'll bring the photographs with me next time. Shall I?"

The front doorbell rings. Noreen. I hear Mrs O'Brien's calm voice. "Goodness. Is that really the time? By all means. I'll tell Mr Connolly you're expecting him home. Straightaway."

Before I leave, Mrs O'Brien gives me a Polo mint. I dawdle down Victoria Avenue. Memories of Mammy are still flooding back.

After our honeymoon, our first home is in Market Drayton. Ash Cottage. Not far from the Post Office. Two happy years there. It might have been longer.

One day a man with a florid complexion comes in the Post Office. Clerical collar. Black suit. Asks the cost of sending a parcel to Liverpool. When I tell him, he says, "A Cork man – if I'm not very much mistaken." I tell him I come from Bagenalstown. Undeterred, he smiles, "Very refreshing hearing the old brogue again." Goes on to give me the times of services in the Catholic Church. Assumes I am a newcomer. Presumes my wife is a Catholic. "I look forward to seeing you and your good lady on Sunday then?" We move soon afterwards. I cannot take the risk. Not now I have Mammy. To Lostwithiel we go. Cornwall. A lovely little Post Office down there.

My teatime visit to Mrs O'Brien, her kindness in listening to me talk about Mammy, has kept me going through many uncertain moments since. Even now, as I lie on my bed suffering from too many prunes, I feel soothed just thinking about it. To have had another person share that with me. Helping me get my feelings out. So that I can begin to grieve. It has helped me to look forward more positively. To accept that life does go on. That it must. That it can still be a rich experience. In July we will all be in Ireland. The welcome will be overwhelming. The hospitality fierce. Declan always had a generous nature. I can imagine it.

Down winding Irish roads in the Ford Anglia. Sean feeling car sick. Cecil concentrating on his compass and map. Noreen handing around sandwiches and cups of soup. Me looking out, not recognising anywhere. Then Bagenalstown. Like any other rural village in appearance. The old house. The church. The school. Smaller than they were. Used by others. Strangers. No doorpost plaques announcing 'Connolly was born here, baptised here, educated here'. A prophet is never honoured in his own land. Not that I ever predicted anything in my life. Apart from the weather. We call in at Byrne's general stores. To use the telephone. Enquire of the operator whether Mr Declan Connolly is on the phone.

"Oh, God, yes. Declan has a phone all right. He's been connected for years."

"Could you connect us, please?"

"Well, no. Not at the present moment. I put a call through to him a few minutes ago. It was his brother Dominic phoning. All the way from Nigeria. Heard him say he might be coming across to stay."

"Oh."

"Wait there... It's Byrne's you're phoning from, no? I will call y'back as soon as they finish talking."

Mrs Byrne, the proprietress of Byrne's Store, gives us cups of tea while we wait. "So you're heading up to Declan's as well? It's lovely there now. Built a house on the hill for Joseph, their son, and his family. Water in the both houses. And electric too... Joseph does all the farm work now of course."

Noreen and Cecil glance at each other. Their expressions seem to say, 'You wouldn't get cups of tea waiting for something in a shop at home.' I hope they are beginning to feel this place is a bit different. I hope they will take it to their hearts.

Sean tells Mrs Byrne he is going to ride on his great uncle's horses. "Ten of them..." She rummages beneath the counter. Finds a packet of sugar lumps. Gives Sean a handful. "For the old nags," she says.

"Hello again, caller." The telephone operator is back. "I am holding Declan Connolly... Putting him through."

"GRE...ATH NEWS. YOU'RE SPEAKING FROM BYRNE'S STORES?" Declan's voice booms down the line. We could probably hear him in person if we stood outside the shop. "CAN YOU COME UP RIGHTH AWAY?... YOU HAVE AN AUTOMOBILE?... THAT'S GRE...ATH. YOU CAN'T COME SOON ENOUGH FOR OUR LIKING."

A cobbled yard. Mud. Straw. Cow dung. Gleann Bheatha Farm. Declan on the doorstep of the original farmhouse. Open arms. Farm dogs tearing everywhere.

"Isn't this greath. GRE...ATH. Come on in, all of yous. Mary's waiting inside." I imagine it to be Mary McDonagh. We greet each other with restraint. Embrace. No words are needed. Nor will be needed. No explanations. The young ones are the important ones now.

Declan moves more slowly than he did. Arthritis has reined his vigorous gait. He keeps a pipe clenched between his few remaining teeth. A habit from a lifetime of outdoors labour. A battered silver lid, full of holes to allow the smoke to escape, protects the bowl of his pipe from the weather.

Declan hugs Noreen warmly. "So you are Noreen, me closest brother's daughter-in-law. What a lovely name. And is this the horseman? We've plenty of horses here for you to try, young sir."

Sean's face lights up. "I've brought them sugar," he shows Declan the sugar lumps disintegrating in his blazer pocket.

Declan steps back. Looks Cecil up and down with an approving eye. Grasps his upper arms. "Cecil. The Civil Servant. Every inch a gentleman, I can see. A pleasure to meet you... I am sure."

Then, with a conjuror's flourish, from rooms all over the house, Declan produces his family. "Me son, Joseph, his wife, Kathleen, their three children, Colum, Francis and Bernadette. Fergus, our other son, Marie, his wife, and their four, Michael, Martin, Desmond and Theresa. Joseph and Kathleen had better hurry if they are going to catch up with Fergus and Marie. Marie is expecting again... God bless her. Our other children and their broods will be along shortly. Now who else have you not seen? Ah, yes. How about this...?" Slowly, from the bedrooms upstairs, emerge John and Mick, my two oldest brothers. Their wives. Their children. Their grandchildren. Sixteen grandchildren altogether.

The rooms downstairs are getting crowded. Mary is busy handing out cakes and cups and cups of tea.

"...And, you won't believe this. Dominic is flying in from Nigeria tomorrow. An even bigger family reunion tomorrow then. Ehh... Wha'about that..?" Declan is beaming. But his brow darkens. "Me only regret is the two youngest. We've not heard from them for years. Manchester, someone said they were living at one time. I just don't know..."

Sean is putting down a saucer of milk for three small, black kittens in the corner of the room. Has made friends with Colum and Francis. They take him outside to dive around in the hay loft and to see the horses.

"You'll take a drop w'us." Declan has glasses and a bottle of something in his huge hands.

"I'll just stick with tea, thanks." Noreen says, looking anxiously at me. I look over to where Cecil stands squashed by friendly relatives against the parlour wall. He signed the pledge at a religious retreat a few years ago but he will usually take one drink on social occasions.

"A very small one, please," Cecil looks relieved to escape from the crush.

Declan pours four fingers of whisky into a pint pot. Cecil accepts it. Too kind to refuse. Declan claps him on the back.

"Sláinte, Cecil. Here's to you and your good lady. She seems to be a fine woman. A striking looking woman too, if I may say so..."

"She's an angel, Declan," I break in, "An angel from heaven. Will we go and have a look around the farm now? Before it gets dark."

Declan suddenly adopts a grave manner. "We will. We will. But let me just say this first. It gives me... unbounded pleasure... to see you all here. Unbounded pleasure. Especially you, Cecil. A nephew I never even knew I had..."

Before we go outside I savour the moment. Sit quietly in a corner on an antique chair of straw and oak. Filled with joy. I have found the Ireland that lived in me through all my years in England and my recent months in Wales. I feel whole. Cecil. Noreen. Sean. Sean's family, if he has one in the future. All can come back here again. Will be welcomed. Can share in this togetherness. I watch Cecil moving around the room. Shaking hands with people. The level of whisky in his glass going down. He seems to be relaxing. My only worry is that Cecil has had so little to do with his roots here. It may be difficult for him. He is such a loyal man. Loyal to his own country. Loyal to his job. His own roots. I cannot turn the clock back. He is what England has made him. What I have made him. What he has made himself. It will be easier for Sean. He has youth on his side. Is at an age when he may enjoy meeting his relatives for the fun they have together. They can write their own history. I will enjoy the visit but it will not be for my benefit. Not for Cecil's. It will be for Sean. May he, Colum, Francis and the others grow close as they get to know each other.

Declan pulls me up out of my chair. "Come and see the farm, my closest brother." I get my stick and hat. He leads me across fields of fine pasture. Points out Joseph's new house, half a mile away up the hill. A small river runs across the lower lying land. On its banks, scrub woodland thrives. Birch trees cast long shadows across the water.

I begin to feel out of place. Declan is wearing thick leather boots. My town shoes and lounge suit would not be ideal wear for haymaking or milking the cows. I nonchalantly pluck a blade of grass. Make a show of chewing on it. Like we did when we worked on the farms together as youngsters. Even spit a few times for good measure. I look up at the clouds gathering over the horizon. "Could be rain," I say, in what I hope is a shrewd tone of voice. A few early raindrops splash down. Fore-runners of the storm to come. We head back to the house. Before we get to the yard I turn to Declan, "You are a lucky man," I say, "but you earned your luck. You had courage."

"And what of you, brother? You have lived in many other places. Been a soldier. Mixed with many people. You have found your own way."

As we walk with difficulty across the cobbled yard Declan has his hand on my shoulder. Still the elder brother.

My imaginings remind me I have to reply to Declan's letter. I move from the bed. Rinse my face over the china bowl. Pour water from the jug over my hands. Wash away the caked, white medicine from my mouth. Dab myself dry with my threadbare towel of faded colours. Find my fountain pen, bottle of ink and Basildon Bond writing paper, behind the old clock. Lay them out on the gate-legged table. Slide a sheet of blotting paper under the ink bottle. Seat myself carefully at the table. Unscrew the top of the ink bottle. Get plenty of ink in the pen. It may be a long letter. Replace the top of the ink bottle. Tear a corner off the sheet of blotting paper. Apply it to the nib of the pen. Soak up excess ink. Want no blots on this letter.

Down Marlborough Hill a brass band strikes up. The Salvation Army. They often come around these streets on Sunday mornings. "...and give us, we pray, peace in our hearts, Lord, at the end of the day..." Peace will always reign between me and my brother. Blood is thicker than water. The pen is mightier than the sword. No time like the present. I must get on and write the letter...

'Dear Declan,

Thank you so much for your kind condolences and sympathy on the sad occasion of Florence's death. It is a great shame she never met you. I am sure you would have got on famously. As I think I mentioned in my letter to you, Florence came from Chester where her parents kept a small hotel. Not a lot in common with yourself at first sight, nor with me for that matter, but Florence had a very kind and gentle nature and a great sense of fun, which I think you would have appreciated...'

Am I writing this for myself? Will any of it make sense to Declan? He cannot picture Mammy. A ladylike English girl is all he would have seen. Not the person I knew and loved through all the years Mammy and I were together.

'...Anyway, brother, to more immediate matters. Cecil, Noreen and Sean were absolutely delighted to receive your invitation to visit, as I was. They cannot wait. It will be their very first visit to Ireland. Sean is looking forward to seeing the river where we used to swim and is desperate to ride a horse (I hope you have one or two?). Cecil is arranging everything at this end. He is so capable. He will be booking some leave from his job in the Civil Service at the start of the school holidays in July. Would a visit at this time be convenient with you? I know summer is a terrible busy time on a farm. Perhaps you and Mary could just let us know whether or not this would suit you.

I cannot find words to express how much I am looking forward to seeing you and the family. It will feel like coming home again in so many ways. Incidentally does my old friend, O'Reilly, still live in the area? And what about his younger brother, Kieran? I don't suppose we would know each other if we met now.

As for myself. I am happy and well looked after. Noreen and Cecil have been wonderful. Taking me to live with them when Florence died. Introducing me to their friends. Taking me on trips. I cannot tell you how good they have been. I have also made some new friends here. One is a widowed lady, born in Sligo. She has a golden retriever with a pedigree as long as your arm. And the local postmaster always has time for a chin-wag. He has introduced me to several places of local interest. Oh, yes, and I've had visits from a young man who tells me he hails from Carlow way, Dermot Pearse. He is very active with the Saint Vincent de Paul Society and a strong Republican. I was wondering if you have ever had anything to do with his family at all? Anyway, enough about me for the time being. I will tell you more when we meet. We have such a lot of catching up to do, don't we?

It would be wonderful, now that we have made contact, if you would consider coming across here later in the year to pay

us a visit. Wales is a beautiful country. I do hope you will.
With love,
Your closest brother.'
It is signed. Sealed. Propped against one of the mandolin
players on the mantelpiece. Sean can post it for me later. That
letter written, our visit feels an important step nearer realisation.
It is great to have it to look forward to. I felt so down for such
a long time, after I wrote to Declan when Mammy died and
received no reply. As soon as Cecil realised, he came up trumps
as usual. It was only a few weeks back. Just as we are finishing
breakfast.

"We are going to London today."
"Are we, Cecil?" You could have knocked me down with a
feather.
"For a trip."
I pack my bag. We are on the road an hour later. I never
knew London was so far away. The A48 all the way to
Gloucester. Then the A40, past Witney, where the blankets
come from, in Oxfordshire. On and on, Cecil drives. He knows
the road all right. Never gets tired. Straight into the heart of
London. It is how I imagine ancient Rome must have looked,
when the power of the Roman Empire was at its height. Vast
stone buildings. Statues of famous soldiers. Whitehall. The
Cenotaph. The Old War Office. Horse Guards in glittering
breastplates mounted on black horses. Powerful men and victo-
rious deeds venerated wherever I look. It is awesome. I think of
people all over the world, the many lives touched by decisions
taken within these buildings. Even my own life. While I wait
with my companions in the trenches before the battle of the
Somme, light-hearted and confident, the War Committee here
in London is already working hard, planning the future direction
of the war. A terrible burden of responsibility they carried. But
we all did our bit for the country. Neither able to function without the other. I notice myself pushing my chest out just a bit
more than usual. Even the paving stones around these buildings
seem steeped in importance. Grooves worn in them by the feet
of so many of the high and mighty down through the centuries.
Cecil points his finger at places I have heard mentioned over

and over again throughout my life. The Treasury. The Cabinet Office. I see them for myself. In all their glory. It is almost a relief to walk down Downing Street. To see the little house the Prime Minister lives in. A terraced house. Number 10. I feel I could tap the little brass knocker and drop in to share a quick cuppa with Mr Macmillan. Tell him how Sean is getting on at school. How generous Cecil and Noreen are to me. Somehow I feel he is the sort of man who will show interest. The friendly policeman at the front door chats away with us. The Prime Minister is not at home today. He is down at Chequers.

Back in the car. The Admiralty. We drive all over the shop. It is a grand little car. Trafalgar Square. Cecil is so kind to arrange all this for me. It is a real tonic. There is the man himself. Up on his column. Admiral Nelson. A real hero, if ever there was one. Kept his nerve to the end at the old Battle of Trafalgar. Whenever it was. So much to remember. So many impressions to take in. I once read poor Horatio used to get seasick at the start of every voyage. A man after me own heart. Not a great traveller myself. I feel a bit queasy as we pull up. What with the long drive. The sightseeing. And Cecil likes to keep the heater on full. To make sure I do not catch a chill.

We are outside a secluded, red-brick building. The Civil Service Club. Just around the corner from the Ministry of Agriculture. I thought we would be putting up at a little boarding house somewhere. Cecil should not be spending all his hard earned money on me. The place is too grand.

"They won't let me in here, will they, Cecil?" Cecil is as cool as a cucumber. Already has the bags. Is half way through the swing doors. I persist. It would be embarrassing to be turned away. Especially for Cecil. Being as he is a Civil Servant.

"Wouldn't we need membership here, Cecil?"

"I am a member," he says. As jaunty as you like.

"But I can't..."

"Yes. Temporary membership. All booked."

"By George. But I'm not..."

"You are. Postmaster. Civil Servant. Retired." Cecil goes off to park the car somewhere safe around the corner.

What an honour. Little did I think I would ever stay at such a prestigious establishment. For self-effacing government servants. Recuperating. Recharging their batteries. Before returning to offices all over Whitehall... London... the world. To foster and protect this great country's interests. Ensuring, by dint of unquestioning loyalty, the smooth turning of the wheels of state. Well, I suppose I played my part all right. Never sent a letter to a wrong address in my life. So far as I know.

I wait respectfully in the foyer. On the wall, above the receptionist's permed head, a large photographic portrait of Queen Elizabeth, the second. A lovely young woman. But so serious-looking. Worried. After just four years on the throne. A beautiful white dress. Diamond-studded tiara. Blue sash. Sovereign of the Most Noble Order Of The Garter. Such a burden to carry on such slender shoulders. All alone. Elizabeth, the second, by the Grace of God, of the United Kingdom of Great Britain and Northern Ireland and of her other Realms and Territories Queen, Head of the Commonwealth, Defender of the Faith. Too many titles altogether. I would have a job just to remember them. The portrait does look grand there though. Like the icon to Our Blessed Lady that used to hang in the old Church in Bagenalstown.

Cecil returns. He addresses the receptionist with great authority.

"Afternoon, Marcia. Rooms?"

"Certainly, Mr Connolly. Two singles. Hot and cold. Tea making facilities and telephones." You can tell she knows Cecil well. "The rooms are all ready for you."

Cecil must have booked everything in advance. Kept it a secret. A wonderful surprise. Such a lot of trouble to go to. Just for me.

"And shall you be requiring dinner, this evening, Mr Connolly?" Marcia asks.

"We shall. In our rooms please."

On the first floor we pass the Ladies and Gentlemens' bathrooms. Polished brass plaques on their mahogany doors. I am in a room next to the mens' bathroom. How thoughtful of Cecil. To think of that.

In my very own room, I enjoy an excellent dinner and sleep better than I have done for donkey's years. The water pipes gush and flow all night in the old bathroom next door. I drop off to sleep dreaming I am a Jack tar on Nelson's flagship at Trafalgar.

Next morning the breakfast tray arrives with a copy of The Daily Telegraph. Cecil thinks of everything. They seem to do exactly what he tells them here. He must be a very important man.

A knock at my door. Cecil himself.

"Westminster Cathedral?"

"Lead on, Macduff," say I.

Cecil has an A to Z guide with all the bus routes.

"Whitehall. Parliament Square. Victoria Street." He works out the route just like that. Leads me to a bus stop opposite the Whitehall Theatre.

From the bus I spot an accusatory brick finger pointing heavenward above the Catholic Piazza. At two hundred yards, the Cathedral's tower makes me want to genuflect, apologise for living, scuttle back to Cardiff. Just when I was beginning to enjoy myself. Cecil is ahead of me. Waves me inside. Buys a cathedral guidebook. Sets off on a tour of inspection.

I rest at the back. It is not an old building. But not modern. Unfinished. Something missing. At eye level, incomplete mosaics glow in the candlelight. Then I notice what is lacking. Up above, where many cathedrals display something dramatic, there is no beauty. No frescoes. No fan-vaulting. All I see is the underside of lofty domes. The stonework looks smoke-damaged, charred. It is like looking into a starless night sky. Lower down, marble. Green. White-veined. Cold.

I have to move. Breathing is becoming difficult. I discover a cheerful side chapel, dedicated to Saint Patrick and all the Irish Saints. A statue of the great man himself hovers in mid air above an altar. Must have some sort of fitting between the wall and the middle of his back. Then a rude reminder of war. A row of plaques commemorates the soldiers of all the British Regiments raised in Ireland. North and South. My own Regiment among them. Nationalism, war and religion, never far apart. An unholy trinity.

Cecil rushes up to me. His face is unusually flushed.

"What achievement! Isn't the Byzantine architecture marvellous. Such ornate richness. It gets better every time I see it." He rushes back to the main aisle and throws himself to his knees as a priest appears on the high altar to celebrate Mass. I follow more slowly. Sit on the bench beside him. Cecil's head is bowed. A large patch of thinning hair is visible on his crown. I have not noticed it before. It seems only yesterday Mammy and I were expressing delight when hair first began to grow there. Mammy used to rub olive oil into Cecil's scalp. To encourage the hair to grow. We decided not to have him baptised as a baby. What with Mammy being Protestant and me not minding either way. We let him make up his own mind when he was older. Mammy said it was important to remember I was baptised a Catholic and the Catholic rule is that the children of mixed marriages should be baptised Catholics. Mammy was so wise. Always tried to do the right thing. When he was about fourteen Cecil chose to be baptised a Catholic.

I whisper in Cecil's ear that I am just popping down to Westminster Abbey. Will take a taxi. To have a quick peep. As I am here. May never get the chance again.

He looks up from his missal, "Westminster Abbey belongs by right to the Benedictines."

"Righto', Cecil," I pat his shoulder, "Back in about half an hour."

Cecil is already concentrating on the Mass again.

"Lord, have mercy. Lord, have mercy. Lord, have mercy.

Christ, have mercy. Christ, have mercy. Christ, have mercy.

Lord, have mercy. Lord, have mercy. Lord, have mercy."

The taxi fare and entrance fee to the Abbey cost me a fair bit out of my pension. But it is worth it. History oozes out of the place. There are more dead Kings and Queens of England in the Abbey than visitors. I cannot help thinking I am surrounded by dead bones. Visitors walk across buried remains. Tomb stones cover so much of the floor. Every other flagstone is a gravestone of some sort. At least those beneath our feet are not forgotten. If that means anything to them now. I cannot resist touching the memorials and tombs. Many before me have done the same, judging by the stonework eroded by nothing more than the glancing touch of hundreds of thousands of fingers. By touching I try to discover a significance I am not feeling. Too many dead. Hard to think of them as flesh and

119

blood. Surrounded by symbols of their wordly wealth and power.

My varicose veins begin to ache. I begin to wish I had stayed quietly on the bench behind Cecil at the Cathedral. At each step I take, my own bones rattle in sympathy with the ghosts of the past. One more side chapel. Glance idly at a trivial monument. A stone urn. My eye is attracted to the inscription. Abbreviated to squeeze it into the available space. I read it half-aloud, "'THIS MONUMNT IS ERECTED TO YE MEMORY OF NICHOLS BAGENALL, (SON OF NICHOLAS BAGE-NALL OF YE IFLE OF ANGLEFEA ESQ: AND OF YE RT. HON.BLE YE LADY CHARLOTT BAGENALL HIS WIFE. ONE OF YE DAUGHTERS OF THE RT. HON.BLE ROBERT LATE EARL OF AYL'SBURY, LORD CHAM-BERLIN; OF HIS MAJESTS; HOUFEHOLD)

WHO WAS BORN YE 31th DAY OF DECEMB: ANNO DOMINI 1687.'"

I read it twice. Could this Nicholas Bagenall be one of the family who gave their name to Bagenalstown? One of those favoured with a gift of Irish lands by a grateful royal patron. Perhaps for military victories achieved in an English Sovereign's name. I have no way of finding out. The verger does not know. Just tries to sell me a brochure about the Abbey. What does it matter anyway? They call it Muine Bheag now. Cecil will be waiting for me. I look again at the lettering closely. Sure, these Bagenalls have two 'L's at the end of their family name. Probably a different family altogether.

The last thing I stumble across is Poets Corner. A tiny niche. Milton, Dryden, Chaucer. Others. At rest. No big statues. Just words. They recite for each other beyond the grave. You can hear them. Just an occasional murmur, if you stand stock still. Even a chuckle. When Chaucer recites. No sign of W.B.Yeats. Eighteen years since we lost him. I bid them all farewell. Hasten back to find Cecil at the Cathedral.

It has been grand. An experience of a lifetime. The Abbey and the Cathedral are both monumental. Memorable all right. Though why two big churches are needed, God himself only knows. They would get a much bigger crowd in if one of them closed down. There is even more competition over at Saint

Paul's. I have no energy left to go on there. Cecil quickly checks his wristwatch as I arrive.

"Buckingham Palace next. Three p.m."

"Suits me, Cecil." I am glad to rest on a bench beside the river for a few hours. Cecil has to attend a meeting around the corner from the Civil Service Club. He leaves me the binoculars. The Parliament buildings are far more impressive than in the picture on the labels of the brown sauce bottles at home. The picture should be much bigger altogether. Amazing stonework. Gothic, according to Cecil's A to Z. I am learning so much. Cecil returns.

"Good meeting, Cecil?"

"Mmmm..."

"That's good."

"Just time. Lunch at the club. Still on schedule. Buckingham Palace. Three p.m."

Cecil finds us a bus. Back to the club. Our club. For lunch in our rooms. Oxtail soup. Roast beef and Yorkshires, carrots, roast spuds, gravy. Jam roly-poly pudding with custard to follow. I have tasted nothing to compare with it since I was in the Army.

"BUCKINGHAM PALACE..." Cecil comes in suddenly as I am dozing off at the table after lunch. Just as well he wakes me. You could hurt yourself badly falling off a dining chair. "Best clothes," he adds.

"In honour of Her Majesty?" I smile. Cecil is so patriotic. He would gladly put his Burberry across a puddle for the Queen to walk on. If she needed it.

I struggle into my best suit. The navy blue one. The bottle green trilby. Always feel comfortable in that. Cecil has brought in a white carnation for my lapel. "To brighten you up," he jokes.

Through Admiralty Arch, we proceed at a stately pace. Cecil decides we need a cab to get us along The Mall in time. It feels as if we are travelling in the golden Coronation Coach. The tourists thronging the pavements, our loyal subjects.

"This do you, pal?" The cab driver drops us off at the main gates to the Palace. The Grenadier Guards march up and down between their sentry boxes. Stamp their feet doing about turns. Smart. Disciplined. I show Cecil how I can still stand to attention. Use my stick as a rifle. Rest it on my shoulder. I march along, taking my lead from one of the guards. A fine six foot four specimen. It brings back the thrill of keeping in step.

"How about this, Cecil? Your old Dad still got a spring in his step, has he?"

"Very good," Cecil says looking back down The Mall. Perhaps he is expecting someone.

I am back on the drill square. 'Square-bashing' we used to call it.

"Left, right. Left, right..." I totter a little. But manage to keep in step with the sentry if I march close behind him.

"Atten... shun," I cry out. Like the old sergeant major. As loudly as I can. I halt. The guard in front of me carries on. I would have liked to continue. But that was enough for the minute. It seemed to be turning into a 'quick step'. The guard takes up his position in front of one of the sentry boxes.

"Well done, mate," I puff, "You're a credit to your regiment." His boots shine like Christmas decorations. "The smartest thing I've seen today." I cannot see his eyes through the bearskin which covers his brow.

"Have y'seen any action, yet? Did they send you to the Suez show, at all?" He is a very quiet man. I see his mouth twitch. Maybe a smile for his old brother-in-arms. Or the bearskin irritating him. They must get awfully hot.

"In the Great War m'self. With a great bunch of lads..."

"He cannot talk. Guard duty. Forbidden." Cecil has given up searching for his friend in The Mall. "Now. Follow me." He sets off at high speed in the direction of a side gate. I notice from my pocket watch that the time is five minutes to three. I do not understand his hurry. We are well within the schedule. Cecil suddenly disappears through the side gate. This is not like him at all.

Cecil looks back briefly. Waves his arms urgently, "Come on. Hurry up."

"Hold your horses," I croak. Hoping the sentry has the bearskin well over his ears.

Cecil has no right to go inside the Palace grounds. He will get us shot.

"I've a surprise for you."

"Another one?" I feel a headache coming on. The jam roly-poly is beginning to repeat on me. This always happens when I doze after my meals. A lot of people in elegant clothes are passing through the same gate into the palace. I follow them inside. I cannot believe it. I am in Buckingham Palace. In the distance I can see Cecil showing a slip of paper to a man at an inner gate. I follow.

"This way for the Not Forgotten Association Garden Party, Sir." The man on the inner gate is hurrying people along. Trying to avoid the queue grinding to a halt.

I am on the camomile lawn before I have a chance to speak to Cecil again. Around us, many old men. Their chests covered in medals. Some, without limbs, in bath chairs. Also younger men. Some sporting handle-bar moustaches. Most with some visible wound or injury. Double breasted blazers with shiny buttons are much in evidence. Military looking badges on the top pockets. Some wear black or maroon berets. Artillery men. Paratroopers. All sorts. Devoted family members cluster around.

"In honour of disabled servicemen from both world wars," Cecil announces in response to my unspoken question.

"Well I'll go to Fishponds." Tears well up in my eyes. "And will she...?"

"Her Royal Highness and Prince Philip will be attending today." Cecil speaks over my head, in the direction of the flourishing beech and plane trees behind me. His back stiffens noticeably as he pronounces the words 'Her Royal Highness'. We wait in a mood of excitement and mounting tension. You would think we were in the depths of the country. The trees make an ideal screen. It takes me back. There were trees like that around the grounds of Recknaw College in Ireland when I was a lad. No traffic noise. Just the occasional clatter of horses' hooves in the courtyard.

In the distance, a splash of yellow stands out like the first crocus of spring. It is Elizabeth, escorted by her tall, handsome Prince. Her Royal Highness looks altogether different from her portrait back at the Civil Service Club. She and the Prince are smiling. Chuckling. Walking close together. Plainly in love. Heading straight for us.

123

"I would have worn me medals if I had known about this, Cecil," I say, trying to blend into the background. The carnation on my lapel makes me look as if I have turned up at the wrong event. I would feel appropriately dressed if we were at a wedding.

"Mmmm..." I definitely detect a hint of panic, even in Cecil's calm manner.

"I have two medals, you know. I was awarded a V.G.C. as well as a War Medal."

Cecil looks impressed, "The War Medal I knew about. I had no idea you were honoured with a V.G.C. too. If only I had known. What does it stand for? Victoria and George Cross?"

"Very Good Conduct! I was kidding y', Cecil. It is just a common or garden Service Medal. Ha Ha Ha. A real big one though. I should be entitled to call myself a V.G.C., wouldn't you say?"

The Queen and The Prince are definitely making a beeline for us. She is probably curious about me hat. No-one else here in a green trilby. At least I have amused Cecil. I can hear him desperately trying to stifle giggles. It is closer to hysteria than laughter. He tries to pretend he is just coughing. Then makes his face look extra serious.

"Sorry about the medals. I wanted the garden party to be a surprise, you see. Told the President of the Not Forgotten Association about your war service, your injuries, to establish your credentials..."

"Don't reproach yourself, Cecil."

"He just sent me the tickets. Told me to turn up. No mention about medals."

My hands are full with a bowl of strawberries and cream and a spoon. My stick hooked over my arm. This will be something to tell Sean and Noreen about. Standing in the warming sunshine, I am day-dreaming vaguely about my first kisses with Mary MacDonagh. Wait. I do not believe it. The Queen really is coming across to speak to us. Suddenly I am so nervous my strawberries and cream are jumping everywhere. Cecil is hopping from one foot to the other. He has gone deathly pale. The next few seconds are the proudest of my life. Equal to what was previously my proudest moment anyway. When I was reserve for the Recknaw College hurling team, winners of the all Ireland schoolboy trophy.

"Good morning. And where have you come from today?" Her Majesty is greeting Cecil. Thinks he is the wounded soldier. It is true. He does not look at all well. Never mind. It will take nothing away from this memory as I go over it time and again in my mind, in the weeks to come. Her manner is so genteel. A real 'gracious' Majesty. She looks stunning. So young and fresh. A yellow suit with tasteful embroidery on the jacket, underlining her bust. A white pearl necklace, matching single pearl ear-rings. Pure white silk gloves. Pure white silk shoes. Her hat. Her crowning glory. Yellow and white fabric petals creating a concoction so light and fluffy it looks good enough to eat.

"Have you come very far?" Her Majesty repeats. She is probably used to people being overawed. Cecil looks as if he has forgotten where we come from. He has.

"Cecil Connolly. Ministry of Agriculture, myself, Ma'am," he is half choking. Caught up, like me, in the emotion of the moment. "My father was the one wounded. At The Battle of The Somme."

Her Majesty's eyes turn towards mine then. They are kindly eyes. Sympathetic. Her expression betrays just slight puzzlement. As if wondering why I am standing so rigidly to attention. I cannot help it. It is my military training. I could not slouch in front of our Monarch if you paid me. Especially with the Guards Band playing for the occasion. 'The Minstrel Boy' is one of my favourites.

"Glad to have you with us today," Her Majesty intones.

"Thank you, M'...Mammy," I stutter, "Sorry, Ma'am, I mean." I grin foolishly.

"Where did you cop it, old man?" The Prince asks bluffly, looking me up and down with a critical eye.

"Where did I... what, sir?"

"Cop your packet? You must have copped a packet somewhere or you wouldn't be here today. Eh, what. Eating all our strawberries and cream up. Ha Ha." What a twinkle the man has in his eye. Her Majesty looks interested to hear my reply.

I squirm on the spot, tongue-tied. My truss creaks gently.

Standing to attention with a bowl of strawberries and cream and a spoon in my hands is a strain.

Cecil taps his ears as if to indicate I am hard of hearing. He leans forward with a confidential air, "Life threatening wound. Lower abdomen, sir. Long recuperation. Slight problems in most areas of physical performance the only legacy these days. Happily."

"COPPED IT DOWN BELOW THEN, OLD CHAP," the Duke shouts. He screws up his eyes, mimicking an episode of intense pain. "WORST PLACE."

Her Majesty performs a similar charade. "WORST PLACE," she opines. How she would know I cannot imagine. "YOU ARE ALL SUCH BRAVE MEN. SUCH BRAVE, BRAVE MEN." The other people at the garden party crane their necks discreetly to see why Cecil and I are getting such high volume attention. Her Majesty moves on to another group like gossamer on a summer breeze.

"GOOD SHOW," the Prince nods vigorously in our direction as he follows his Queen. "DAMN FINE SHOW. SEE YOU AGAIN NEXT YEAR, I HOPE."

Cecil's lower lip is quivering. His chest is heaving, "Albert Memorial." His words gush out. "Last visit. Then home."

"I'll never forget this, Cecil. Thank you." I shake Cecil by the hand. In Buckingham Palace. On the camomile lawn.

After the elation of meeting the Queen and the Prince, our visit to the Albert Memorial is a sad contrast. I feel so sorry for Prince Albert. Sitting all alone. Ever since his monument was completed in 1876. Holding nothing but a catalogue for the Great Exhibition. Waiting patiently for Victoria to come to him. Her statue, when the time came, found its way to another part of London. He should be holding her in his arms, not the old catalogue. It would have been what they wanted.

It is an exciting week. On the Saturday after we get back from London, I have a win on the football pools. There are very few score draws that week. The radio announcer predicts a bumper payout.

I get Noreen to book the family into The Sully Inn for a celebratory meal. In the pages of the South Wales Echo, I scan through the motor dealers. The cars I saw in London are still on my mind. Every other one a Jaguar, Rover or a Daimler. Rolls Royces ten a penny. I can see Cecil in a Rover. He will have one. A car in keeping with his station in life.

I give Noreen double lodgings money that week.

"And that's just for starters, Noreen." I fold the bank notes up, small. Press them into the palm of her hand. Fold her fingers around them. So she will not realise how much is there until she unwraps the notes. I wink conspiratorially. "Your kindness does not go unnoticed. I am going to see you all right, all right." I am bursting to tell her about my Pools win but I keep it a secret until I know how much I have won.

"Been drinking again, Pop? Remember what I said. Treat your stomach lining with respect... it will treat you with respect..." Noreen does not falter in her Hoovering. Pushes the money almost brusquely into her apron pocket. She is going to get such a surprise when I tell her.

The meal at The Sully Inn is a great success. It is much nicer down there in the summer. Noreen has always said it is expensive. She is quite right. But that is exactly why I want to take them there. To treat them. We have the works. Champagne. Laver bread. Mints with the coffee. Our plates are brought in covered with silver domes. At the appointed moment, waiting staff whisk them off with a flourish. I have never seen anything like it. This is how we shall live all the time from now on. The portions of food beneath the domes are small. It has to be said. Compared to Noreen's meals. But it forces us to eat tiny amounts on our forks. To chew slowly. In a refined manner. I pay the bill. Borrow the money from Cecil, of course. For the time being. Will repay him a hundredfold when the money comes through. The faces of the family are radiant in the light from the candelabra which grace the centre of the table. It is a memorable moment and calls for a few well-chosen words.

"I would like you to think of this meal as a little thank you, from me... for everything." I look steadily at Noreen, Cecil, and Sean in turn before raising my champagne glass high and drinking deeply to the health and happiness of, "...The family." It is the only way I can get the taste of the laver bread out of me mouth. No-one told me it was seaweed from West Wales, until after I had eaten it. The rest of the meal is, as they say, fit for a king.

When we get home, I fish from my pocket the coins I got in change when I paid the bill. Six pennies. Place them on the mantelpiece in my room. A few days later Sean is with me. I hold up one of the pennies, in front of him.

"Who is that, Sean?"

"Britannia..."

"Good lad. And Britannia is?"

"Britain pers... personified."

I turn the coin over.

"And who is this fine fellow?"

"George the sixth," Sean replies in a flash. Keen as mustard.

"Good boy. Our present Queen's father."

"The one with a brother who... eradicated?"

"Abdicated. Excellent. Keep learning your kings and queens, Sean. It's a must, if you live in England."

"I live in Wales, grandad."

"So you do, lad. Anyway here's six pennies for your money box."

Sean tosses the pennies into a round box which used to hold toffees. "That's half a crown I've got now," he smiles up at me.

"Half a crown, eh? As much as that! It will be a lot more before too long, if your old grandad's got anything to do with it."

"Are you rich, grandad?" Sean is tucking his money box away in my sideboard.

"No, Sean. But I might be soon." He was the only one I told that much to.

Five score draws. Three no score draws. Eight draws altogether. Twenty one points. The most I ever had. The following Tuesday I receive a cheque for two pounds seven and six.

Having your health and a loving family around you are worth more than any pools win. Thousands of pounds cannot buy happiness. That is what I tell myself. What I say to Cecil when I can no longer put off explaining to him that it will take me a couple of months to repay the cost of the meal. Deep inside I know what satisfaction it would have given me, to buy Cecil a Rover. To be able to help out more than I do. I have tasted how good it feels.

The effort of writing the letter to Declan has taken it out of me. I lay me down on the bed again. Rest. Try not to excite myself. It is no good. I have been like it all my life. I cannot feel easy until a thing is done. Otherwise it preys on my mind. I am the same with people. If I take a shine to someone, I want to be with them all the time. I fall in love with everyone who is kind to me. After taking tea with Mrs O'Brien, images of her drift before me all the time. The sound of her voice lingers in my ears. Full of longing and wistfulness... "In a field by the river my love and I did meet..." I hanker after a whiff of the eau de Cologne or whatever it is she dabs behind her ears. I am convinced she must feel for me as I do for her. Somewhere inside. Even if she finds it hard to admit it. Maybe she thinks love is undignified at our age. Not that I mean we should rush things. Just cement our friendship. I am desperate to see her. I resort to every possible means to spend time in her company. Even devious. With limited success.

The Thursday after my visit to Mrs O'Brien's. The day we collect our pensions. I crane my neck to spot her as she emerges from Victoria Avenue, turns down Marlborough Hill. The trigger for action. I already have my wooing outfit on. Since the Buckingham Palace garden party, I have taken to wearing my regimental tie more often, with the navy suit and trilby. I have dug out my war medals from the pocket in my suitcase and often wear them around the house now. Noreen says I would look silly walking down Marlborough Hill in them. So I have not done that yet.

Mrs O'Brien is crossing the road. High heels. At her age. They ring out so proudly. It is great. Paddy is not with her today. That is a relief. I am down the stairs like a tortoise after a dose of the old liver salts.

"Bye, Noreen. Off to get me pension," I shout along the hallway and manage to close the front door behind me before Noreen has a chance to reply.

129

I am down the front steps so fast I bang right into the front gate before I can open it. That wastes precious seconds.

Across Victoria Avenue I dance, slithering and sliding a bit on the loose gravel as I go. It is a day to rejoice in. The sun beats down. I can smell the tarmac. The tang of disinfectant on the front steps of number 198. The aroma of freshly baked bread wafting up the lane from the Turog bakery. I am catching up with Mrs O'Brien. She has two of the finest, most muscular buttocks I have ever seen. Round and smooth like the Kerry hills. What style. Her tight skirt is in dark green tartan. She turns in at the Post Office at the foot of Marlborough Hill.

The door fights hard to keep me out. I force it open, breathing hard. My reward is a seductive waft of Mrs O'Brien in place of the usual musty mail sacks and brown envelopes. Angus is already complimenting Mrs O'Brien on her appearance while counting out and handing over her pension.

"I've alweeys had greet fondness for the tartan, you nooo. Especially wrapped around a woman of greet beauty..."

You would think he would know better. Him, a married man, with three children.

Mrs O'Brien looks pleased to have been noticed by the craggy Scot. He who hesitates is lost. I make my presence known.

"Good morning, Angus..." I nod to Angus. Then turn to Mrs O'Brien as if surprised to see her there.

"Oh, it's yourself, Mrs O'Brien. I didn't recognise you from the back."

"Good day, Mr Connolly. In your regimental tie I see. Very distinguished indeed."

I knew it. She does like me. A little at least. If I had my medals on who knows what effect they would have had. I press home my advantage.

"And you, Mrs O'Brien, if I may be so bold, look as fresh as a parma violet."

She blushes charmingly. Still has a great air of innocence about her.

"You flatterers. I must rush now. My nieces are waiting for me up at the house."

She is here. She is gone. All at once, the Post Office looks different. Ordinary. Its floor of chequered black and white tiles, its cream painted walls, the bare light bulb dangling from a fraying flex, damp patches on the ceiling. The fire which illuminated and transformed the place two minutes ago has sputtered and died. Such is the effect of Mrs O'Brien's departure. I approach the counter to collect my money. Angus is rocking with silent laughter. One hand covers his mouth. The other is pointing at me.

"Did ye not ken what ye were saying...?" It is a few minutes before Angus manages to get any more words out. At last he manages to stand up straight again.

"Parma violets are these little things here..." He shows me a box of small purple sweets in twists of cellophane.

My legs become restless. I hate lying in bed during the day. The bed clothes get rucked up. A sense of dread creeps over me. How can I dwell on Mrs O'Brien's physical attractions like this? Mammy not yet in the ground one year. It cannot be right. I force myself to think of Mammy. Was never tempted to stray while she was alive. Our love was complete. Through all those years. It meant everything. Yet since I lost her there is a sense of release. I have to admit it. The delicious thrill, which freedom bestows, invades me. I have not been used to it. I am a young man again. In my mind anyway. I need not feel guilty. Mammy will always be Mammy. She knows me better than to think anything can ever diminish what we had. What I still have. Still I feel as if something awful is going to happen I cannot settle. I turn over, but now my underblanket has shifted. I am disturbed by several hard, mattress buttons. I face my own thoughts at last. My dread is about the possibility that I will not be well again by Thursday. That I could miss my weekly visit to the Post Office. Miss seeing Mrs O'Brien. So be it. I have a great affinity with her. But life with Mammy was peerless.

Mammy sits in the lee of the fuschia bush, beside our back porch in Burnham-on-Sea. She has the deckchair out. On her lap an apron of newspaper, carrots and potatoes in a colander. She peels the vegetables for our evening meal. The sun is shining steadily. Her face is tanned. Dark brown. So unlike later on. Sean is staying with us, while his mother and father tour the West Country.

Down the centre of the garden is a thin strip of lawn. On both sides, fruit bushes, herbs, vegetables of all sorts, flower beds in full bloom.

Sean is up at the top end, gathering pea pods for Mammy. The brown paper carrier bag is half-full already. Near him, I sit on my bench gazing over the garden fence into the meadow beyond the garden. Fresian cows are grazing there. They come right up to the fence. Curious. Unsure what I want. It is time for the farmer to take them in for milking. I see him coming across the field to round them up.

Sean and I make our way back along the garden path. Sean with the bag of peas for Mammy. I teach him part of a song I learned in my youth. "To be a farmer's boy..." I cannot remember the rest. Sean sings it with a will.

"TO BE A FARMER'S BOY..."

I sing with him. We do not care that we only know part of it. We sing the same fragment over and over.

Mammy chuckles at Sean's enthusiasm.

"You'll make a farmer out of him yet, Pop."

"He'd be a champion farmer, too."

Mammy looks thoughtfully at him.

"What do you want to be, when you grow up, Sean?"

"..Be a fireman," he says, unhesitatingly.

Happy days. Mammy and me together. Approaching retirement. Our little grandson full of life. Secure. Loved.

What I remember best is Mammy and me talking to each other. About the day. What people have said to us at the Bowling Club. How nice it has been down at the beach. The vividness of a sunset. Sometimes sharing silence. But usually chatting away sixteen to the dozen. About anything and everything. I miss it in the evenings most of all. Being able to talk with Mammy.

I love to converse. I like to sit and think. But most of all I like to talk. That is why I enjoy Sean's company so much. He listens to me. Boring old tripe it must seem at times. And I like hearing what he has to say. He can prattle with the best of them. Has his own slant on things. Fresh ideas. A mind of his own. I like that. He can get his own way too. But he uses charm, not bullying. At Easter, he set his heart on swimming in Llandaff Fields open air swimming pool.

"Do you feel like a walk, Grandad?"

"Mebbe..." I am suffering from a corn on my little toe and have no corn pads.

"Not too far. Just up the hill, along Pencisely Road, Palace Road, Howells Crescent, to Llandaff Fields and back."

"No distance, then?"

"You can do it, Grandad." Sean really seems to believe I can.

"Go ahead, Sean. I am your man." It is hard to refuse him.

We are the only customers at the pool. The pool attendant is barricaded inside his kiosk. A wooden board is in place behind the window where you pay. I knock briskly. The man peers out, clearly surprised to see people.

"One junior swim, one spectator, please." I hand him a ten shilling note. Inside the kiosk, I can see a teapot on the table beside a half-full mug of steaming tea. An electric fire warms the attendant's feet. I rub my hands. Cup them together. Blow warm breath into them.

The pool attendant holds the ten shilling note in mid air.

"You sure?" he says, looking at Sean. "It's not heated, you know."

"I like it cold," he replies bravely. "And I've always wanted to have the pool to myself." Sean hurries off to change.

It is like standing on January lino, on that poolside. The sky is heavy with grey cloud. A sharp breeze is blowing upstream from Tiger Bay along the nearby River Taff. The water in the pool looks ice blue. Ripples slapping hard between the side of the pool and the silver hand-rail.

The pool attendant takes pity. Invites me inside. Pours tea for me. He is a talker too. Gets lonely in his kiosk at this time of the year. Tells me his name is Demosthenes. He is a Greek Cypriot. Loves talking about the land. As I do. Tells me all about how quickly his tomatoes used to grow on Cyprus. The richness of the olives there. How he used to rub olive oil on his skin to protect it. Never burned. He loves the television too. Wells Fargo. Cheyenne. Opportunity Knocks. He offers me a Players cigarette. As always I am reminded of my first meeting with Mammy, the mirror with Players Please on the top, in which I saw Mammy watching me. For a moment I fall silent. Then I recover. Tell Demosthenes This Is Your Life is my favourite. The way Eamon Andrews just stands there. The book open in his hands. Going through the subject's life. In the space of half an hour. I go through it all with them. Weep from beginning to end. More than ever I have about my own life. The people always seem to have done so much. Endured so much. Given so much to others. Eamon Andrews is a clever fellow. Started on the radio. Commentating on boxing matches. Demosthenes, like Sean and myself, has been following the career of a local Cardiff boxer. Joe Erskine. British and British Empire heavyweight champion. A brilliant boxer. An artist. No knockout punch. All skill and a big heart. When he gets knocked down, he gets right back up again. His bravery is beyond question. I was inspired to give Sean some advice after one of Joe's fights.

"It's like in life, Sean," I said wisely. "You get knocked flat but you have to keep getting up and starting again." I was a great one to talk, I thought afterwards. Have spent most of my life getting stretchered off, moving on, avoiding things. But I wanted to prepare Sean. Help him to deal with things when they did crop up, as I knew they would even if he did not.

"Shouldn't the boxers get better first, Grandad? Before they get up...?"

"Well, they are given ten seconds to recover, so they are..." My words peter out. I see he is right. No-one can say. Maybe sometimes it is better to be like a reed bending in the breeze or a flower of the field neither toiling nor spinning.

Sean is out on the pool side. Swinging his arms. Teeth chattering with excitement and cold already. He steps straight up to the diving tables. His little legs can only just stretch from one to the other. The top table is about the same height as the ceiling in the lounge at home. A quick breath and in he goes. More like a stone dropping than a dive. Up quickly. Arms threshing the water. Hair flat on his head. Cheeks puffed out. Eyes wide. Concentrating fit to bust. Straight to the bank. Up the steps.

On our way home, Sean speaks for the first time.

"Did you see my dive, Grandad?"

"I did."
"Was it any good?"
"It was brilliant, Sean."

My lips are dry. Noreen advised me not to drink anything for the rest of today. It would give me the runs worse. I take another spoon of Kaolin and Morphine. I am not sure how many that is. I have a raging thirst. As bad as I had in the hospital tent at The Somme. Fancy I have a bit of a fever. I hope Noreen will bring me some tea soon.

The Somme is not too bad at first. A few shells overhead and patrols in No Man's Land but no big engagements. I am part of the build up of British forces on French soil, before the battle. The Germans know they are up against it when they get word, too late, that they now have me to reckon with. Unfortunately, they do not panic or retreat in disarray. So I take my place in the trenches. On the Continent for the first and only time in my life. Well pleased with myself. Then news comes through of the Easter 1916 Uprising in Dublin. The rebels in the Post Office in O'Connell Street. The brutal suppression of the uprising and execution of the ringleaders. It does not hit me at first. I think how sad the loss of life is, of course. I assume it will only be a matter of time before things settle down and return to normal. For some reason it takes German soldiers to bring the full significance of those events in Dublin home to me. The Germans know there are Southern Irishmen in our trench, just opposite their front line. They shout over to us.

"The English are murdering your countrymen in Dublin... Come over and join us... Come on... Fight with us against the murderers..." I realise then. It is not going to stop. I can never go back to my village in Ireland. They know there which army I have been in. Will see me as an enemy of Home Rule. A murderer by association. My hopes of ever returning to Mary MacDonagh and bringing her away with me are finally destroyed. For a time I feel deep despair. Unable to go back home. Trapped in the Army. At the front. Risking my life. But severed from the one I am risking my life for.

Then the time comes to give Fritz a bloody nose. I am almost relieved that something is to happen at last. First, seven days of shelling the German positions to soften them up and to clear the barbed wire out of our way. Then, at last, July 1st, 7.30am. Over the top. The Big Push. I am a signaller. My job is to follow our troops advance with a large drum of signal wire. Soon discover why they call it the Big Push. Shove the signal wire a third of a mile, up a slight slope, all on my own. Through heavy enemy machine-gun fire. I push for all I am worth. I know how important it is for our Officers to establish a telephone link between captured German trenches and our H.Q. at the rear.

British soldiers are spinning to the earth on all sides of me, like skittles in a one-sided skittle game. I push and crawl. Push and crouch. Push and... finally decide something is badly wrong with my lower belly. I know not what. I just know it has all been too much for my young muscles. I struggle on. Manage to set up the line.

Later, I have to work back along the cable to repair sections damaged by the shelling. At one stage I find myself lying in a shell-hole under heavy fire, with other British soldiers. Some are taking cover. Some are wounded. Some dead. I feel no fear. Death can come. I have little to lose. Perhaps I should have tried to feel more fear. Around me, the other survivors are cowering down, covering their faces with their arms, mumbling and groaning.

I crawl back to our position in the forefront of the attack. I have to report to H.Q. on our progress, the strength of the German resistance, casualties, and also receive orders from H.Q. My mind is as clear as a bell as I send off the reports. I am convinced God is at H.Q. and I am the only one able to put him in the picture. 'FORWARD POSITION SECURED... SINE CURA... SHELL BURST BRIGHT... FIRES IN THE FIRMAMENT... MACHINE GUN POST... RIGHT.' In the trench, a soldier runs past me screaming. The back of his head gone. 'OH, NO... IT IS GONE... JUDGEMENT DAY IS COME... VENGEANCE IS... SALVE... WOUNDS... SALVE REGINA... SALVATION... THE WAY OF THE CORPS... ANTISEPTIC... OINTMENT... ANOINTED FLESH... CASUALTIES... HANGING ON... THORNS...

UNDERFOOT... UNBOWED...' I know my job is to keep the messages going.

'PULL YOURSELF TOGETHER, MAN.' A voice barks down the line. Another man brushes against me, bewildered, blood pumping from his shoulder, his throat. A shrapnel wound. He starts to haemorrhage from the mouth. My message goes out without hesitation.

'WINE COMES IN AT THE MOUTH
AND LOVE COMES IN AT THE EYE;
THAT'S ALL WE SHALL KNOW FOR TRUTH
BEFORE WE GROW OLD AND DIE.
I LIFT THE GLASS TO MY MOUTH,
I LOOK AT YOU, AND I SIGH.'

My mind is shutting it out. Reciting poems. Such incongruous nonsense. Yet I believe I am doing a great job. Someone has to report back from hell. God is counting on me. A runner is sent up from H.Q. to replace me. The Captain in charge has a look at my hernia. Tells me I have to go back. To a casualty clearing station. I reply, desperate to be a hero, "I can carry on, sir. Don't want to miss any of the show..." He gets stretcher bearers to take me. They are under the impression that I have a serious stomach wound. Need urgent surgery. I am too busy pointing out the angels flying overhead to put them right. They leave me in the corner of an Operating Tent which is full of men with arms and legs blown off, blinded, entrails exposed. Men dying. Too ill to scream.

I was one of the lucky ones. Not that I thought so at the time. Would have given anything to have got through the battle. To play my part. Though it took a while to achieve anything there. I would have been lucky to get through it if I had not been invalided out.

I never wanted to see war again, afterwards. Once I had the time to think about it. You met and heard of others who felt the same. A man in the hospital back in Blighty told me of a Dublin Professor he met on the first of July 1916. An ardent Irish Nationalist, the Professor was deeply affected by what he saw on that first day of battle. Resolved to work for a peaceful settlement of the Irish Question when he got back to Ireland. The next day his head was blown off by a stray enemy shell.

On the far side of my bedroom is a police officer wearing the uniform of the Irish Garda. He has chosen to put himself at the gate-legged table. Sits very upright, formal. I feel too hot and thirsty for all this. At a disadvantage, lying in bed. He points to a sheet of paper lying on the table.

"Purpose of visit... Intended destination... Length of stay..." He purses his lips with an air of self-importance. "We need all that filled in properly." He stares at my War Medals, which I have left carelessly lying on the mantelpiece, before speaking again. "I noticed a Union Jack pennant on the Ford Anglia outside. Anything to do with you?"

I try to call for Noreen but my throat is paralysed.

"That is all I require just now, sir. Please remain where you are." As if I am going anywhere. "There is someone else with more to say to you." He bows stiffly. As he opens the door, he spots the holy water font Cecil has put up next to the light-switch. He scribbles on the form. Dips his finger in the water. Crosses himself. Leaves.

President Eamon De Valéra is next in. Sprawls informally on the end of the bed. I have to lever myself up on my elbows to see him.

"Sure, you'll be all right, Connolly. The Garda are just doing their job. Y'know how 'tis."

I nod eagerly. Glad that the great man has such an understanding attitude to my plight.

"They have dropped the odd bollock, y'know. In the past."

I nod again.

"Tightening up now. Well, we had to struggle so hard, y'see. Parnell'd tell y'the same. So many gave up their lives for the cause. Despite the back-sliders. Which reminds me. Where was our man, Connolly, when he was needed?"

I make a gesture of helplessness. Arms outstretched.

"And now y'want to pay us a social visit, when everything's rosy in the garden." His voice hardens just a little. "We still have partition y'know. It's not plain sailing. What d'yous have to say to that?"

My eyes search the ceiling for inspiration. All I see is a few old cobwebs. The President is becoming impatient with me, I can tell.

"Wait there." All of a sudden, he is a man of action. "An old friend of yours is outside. Still sees your school chums. Wants a quiet word."

Brother Benignus creeps in without a sound. I notice he is playing with the leather strap which he keeps in his pocket. Stands on Mammy's hearthrug, his back to the electric fire.

"They tell me the prodigal intends to return, Connolly."

I am getting used to nodding.

"Never could understand why y'left us, young man. Y'had a good brain. A good home. Lived in a lovely village. Had a fine career ahead of you, if y'd stayed." He casts his eyes down as he continues. "Someone told me one time, y'had a beautiful fiancée there too."

I put on an expression meant to imply I loved it there but I really had to leave. Benignus sighs. I take him to imply, in his turn, that some people in this world will never learn.

"Anyways, this proposed visit. I would counsel caution. I say no more than that. Think twice, Connolly. Remember the O'Reillys. The poor mites. That younger boy, Kieran. He's a brute of a man now. You'd not want to cross him. He has some very funny ideas. I would definitely stay away if I were you..."

At last I find my voice.

"Th.. ank you f.. f.. for calling, Brother."

Brother Benignus has not changed a bit. I hear him strap the banisters as he flies down the stairs without a sound. How he misses the steps which creak near the bottom is a miracle. He has never been to the house before.

Hasty, heavy footsteps ascend. Thank god, it must be Noreen. Yeats himself sweeps in.

"I've not got long. Maud is waiting downstairs. I'm in with a chance at last. She's agreed to stroll in the park with me afterwards."

It is not every day that you meet a colossus. I want to help him if I can.

"I can recommend the park up Victoria Avenue, there. Only two and a half minutes walk. Pond, fish, statue. Lovely on a sunny day."

"Thank you, old boy, but no. My destiny is to spend a wine-dark midnight in the sacred wood with her."

139

Who am I to quibble? He must have a cottage somewhere up in Leckwith Woods. Knows Cardiff quite well then. Would not fancy that myself. Stumbling over tree roots in the dark.

"Surely you will stay for a cuppa? Please do. I have admired your poetry for so many years. Perhaps Maud would like a cup, too?"

"No, no. We really must not dally. I just wanted to say this. Take no notice of the President, the guard, the little fellow with the strap. I saw them leaving. Arm in arm. Heading for a licensed premises down the road. Don't know their axis from their elbow. Sure they don't. Don't let them frighten you."

"You think I should visit my brother?"

"Make your journey. Just remember – all perform their tragic play. You as much as the next man. And why not, indeed? The great stage curtain about to drop... get in there man. Talk to the old family in Bagenalstown. You will find they don't give a toss any more. It's all more or less sorted as far as they're concerned in the South of the country."

"It's safe to take the family over?"

"We poetry lovers must stick together. Trust each other. Take my advice. Go. Do not delay. Make your journey. This is no dress rehearsal. This is the real thing. We shall not pass this way again."

He sounds like Angus down in the Post Office. They certainly both have philosophical leanings. I wonder if Angus writes poetry too.

"...All things fall and are built again... Civilisations... Empires... Military strength..."

The man has a tongue of gold.

'The Incas, The Ancient Egyptians, The Greeks... Romans... Spanish... English... French. Nothing endures. You, yourself, are acquainted with the military might of the German Army, I believe? Though it did not prevail, thanks to the unswerving valour of such lion hearts as yourself..."

Now he is enjoying himself. Has forgotten all about Maud. I hand Yeats my precious first edition copy of his poems.

"Please sign this. Before you go..."

The famous poet looks pleased. Even at a tribute so small.

"...there's a fountain pen behind the clock on the mantel-piece."

With a flourish Yeats writes on the flyleaf, 'To Conoly, Traveller to Byzantium extraordinaire. W.B. Yeats.' His spelling is no better than my brother Declan's. He is not yet finished.

"I'll tell y'something I've not told many people, Connolly."

"Are yous sure you want to?"

There is something excitable about him now.

"Yes. I want you to know that big changes are afoot. Christianity has provided mankind with nearly 2,000 years of obedience, pity, chastity and self-abnegation, before an abstract and rigid God. It is running out of steam. The Christian era was begun by a virgin birth. During the classical era, the virtues of beauty, aristocracy, sexual prowess and heroic splendour of conduct were prized. It began with a swan's rape of a girl, according to Leda and the Swan..."

The man is as mad as a hatter. All I want is rest. I wish he would go.

"...Each age differs from the previous one. The era that will annihilate Christian virtue will come in A.D. 2,000. A turbulent and energetic new world will be summoned into being by the mass imagination of the human race, out of our own rich experience..."

"How interesting. Thank you for sharing that with me, Mr Yeats."

"Call me William Butler, do."

To my relief, William Butler suddenly notices the time. Rushes down the stairs calling, "MAUD... MAUD-Y... WHERE ARE YOU MAUD-Y... YOU HAVEN'T GONE, HAVE YOU?.. BEGORRA... SHE HAS TOO..."

A gentle knock on my door. Who now? The Pope himself?
Noreen. Thanks be.

"How's the tum?"

"Empty, Noreen."

"I've brought some nice, dry toast. Just to start you off."

"Any chance of a drink, at all?"

Noreen finds the glass soda siphon down beside my comfy
chair. A great thick thing. The precious fluid bubbles freely up
the central stem. Gushes out. Noreen quickly takes her hand off
the lever. An inch of soda water fizzes in my tumbler. Its sides
are opaque. I have not rinsed it lately. I am ashamed. Will wash
it properly when I am on my feet again.

"No more treks to Mass for you, Pop. It is simply too far."

"Will y'tell Dermot, I cannot manage the van steps either?"

"I will."

"Thanks, Noreen."

You can rely on Noreen. She has great strength.

"Get this down you. Then rest."

Noreen leads with a straight left jab. A dessert spoon full of
Kaolin and Morphine in her hand.

"I've already... GULLLM. That'll settle it Noreen. I don't
think the runs'll bother me this night."

I ask her to get Sean to post my letter to Declan. She looks
pleased I have replied. Her serious expression eases.

"I am really looking forward to Ireland."

She has not had a decent holiday for so long. It costs a lot
putting Sean through his school. Then there is the mortgage on
the house. Entertaining friends. And I probably cost more to
keep than I contribute. What with trips out. The cost of petrol.
A holiday will do them all good.

Noreen tucks my blankets in tight on both sides. Squeezes my
hand. Lowers the venetian blinds. Draws the curtains. I stop her
before she goes.

"Did we have visitors earlier, Noreen?"

"No. Why?"

"No reason... I just wondered."

I watch Noreen in the doorway. I do not want her to go. The landing light glows softly all around her.

"Do you need a passport for Ireland, Noreen?"

"I don't think so. No, I am sure you don't."

"God bless, Noreen."

"Sleep well, Pop."

When Noreen has gone downstairs, I wrestle myself free of the blankets. Tread carefully across the room. Knees bent, to keep my balance better when I bump into the furniture. Hands on the backs of chairs for support. I relish the springiness of the hearthrug beneath my feet when I reach it. I retrieve my medals from the mantelpiece. Collect Declan's letter off the sofa. Put them both on the bed. Open the battered suitcase which I keep beside Mammy's hatboxes, underneath the bed. I place my medals and Declan's letter in the pocket of the suitcase where I keep my brown scapula, Mary MacDonagh's last letter, and a picture of Mammy and me which we had taken during our honeymoon in Porthmadog. I push the suitcase back under the bed. Remain on my knees for several minutes. Not in prayer. Just dizzy. Back into bed. The bedclothes are tangled up again. No matter. The medals will be better off in the suitcase. I would not want too many people to see them. They could easily get stolen.

I do not notice myself going to sleep. When I wake I feel anxious. A lot is on my mind. How will Cecil pay for the trip to Ireland? Surely he cannot afford all that money. The cost of the ferry. The meals. The petrol. Presents for all Declan's family over there. And who will look after the house here? It will not be safe. You read so much about burglary in the papers. I feel sweat on my neck. Sweat in the stubble on my chin. I must do something. Persuade them not to go. It is a matter of urgency. But Noreen wants to go. They all do. I must warn them. Alert them to the danger before Cecil buys the tickets. Mrs O'Brien will help me. She will know what to do.

Up Victoria Avenue, I am surprised to see most of the street

143

lights still on. At this hour. The clock in my room said it was two o'clock. Not a soul around. The world is going mad. They should all be up and doing. I knock on Mrs O'Brien's door.

"Mr Connolly. What are you doing out in your pyjama trousers?"

"Pyj..? Yes, I am. I just got out of bed..."

I could say the same about her, mind you. Not dressed herself yet. Two o'clock in the afternoon. There she stands in her maroon velvet dressing gown and hairnet. Proud as Punch.

"It is two in the morning, sir."

She looks very disapproving. Has not grasped the importance of my visit at all.

"You must listen. We have got to help them. Their house could be broken into... and where will they get the money? Cecil just cannot afford it. It is so awful. I am so worried..."

"What is all this about, Mr Connolly?"

"Noreen and Cecil, and poor little Sean. They are planning to go across to Ireland... the cost... much too much... they must be helped... stopped... I just don't know what to do..."

"Come, come. Let's discuss it in the morning."

I notice Paddy sloping along Mrs O'Brien's hallway. Not too pleased at being woken. Best to leave it until the morning then. Mrs O'Brien takes me by the arm. Guides me back down the Avenue.

Cecil appears cautiously, in response to Mrs O'Brien's fusillade of knocks on the front door.

"I've got to talk to you, Cecil..." I blurt.

"In the morning, Mr Connolly. In the morning." Mrs O'Brien has such a soothing way with her. She pats me on the arm. I almost expect to hear the command – 'sit' – at any moment. I would if she asked me to. Instead she addresses herself to Cecil again, "Mr Connolly has been for a wander. Found him outside my house about five minutes ago. He seems a little confused." Behind Cecil, Noreen appears. She is in a hairnet too. I am not the only one in my nightclothes then. Not by a long chalk.

"Are you feeling all right, Pop?" Noreen asks with concern.

"Me bowels are as right as rain since the medicine, Noreen. It's grand stuff. Would recommend it to anyone."

"Good night, all." Mrs O'Brien is off up the Avenue in that maroon dressing gown still. Has the woman no shame?

After all the fuss, I am glad to get back to bed.

At eight o'clock, I wake again. I know it is morning because daylight is streaming in through chinks in the curtains and blinds. I try to sit up. Fall back on my pillows. Feeling ill. My strength has gone. I need to use my chamber pot. I bang my walking stick as loudly as I can on the floor, to alert Cecil. He has not gone off to work yet. I hear him singing Saint Therese Of The Roses in the kitchen.

It helps me understand how frustrating for her Mammy's illness must have been. Never complained once.

Unable to drink without help. I hold her porcelain drinking cup to her mouth. It has a spout like a little teapot, to drink through. Helps her to drink without spilling anything on the covers.

The nurses are very good. Come into the house in Burnham-on-Sea several times every day. But Mammy likes me to sit with her through many of the hours between their visits. It is the least I can do. I make the room as nice as I can. Bunches of chrysanthemums from the flower shop down the road. No flowers left in the garden. Embroidered cushions from the living room for the two chairs which I have moved into our bedroom. For their colour.

Mammy often asks me to read to her. Anything and everything. Novels. Magazines. Newspapers. Much of the time her eyes are fixed on my face. A distant expression in them. It is mainly the sound of my voice she wants. To know there is someone near.

It is October. The month before she died.

"Listen to this, Mammy, what it says in The Times. A report from Dar Es-Salaam. The Princess is there... 'So crowded was Zanzibar's mile long seafront this morning that hundreds of people stood knee-deep in the water on the narrow golden beaches to greet Princess Margaret when she arrived in the island for her three day visit...' How about that?"

Today her eyes sparkle and dance as if she is picturing herself among the crowds in the sunshine, surf splashing between her toes, awaiting the Princess's arrival.

"'Later, at the palace, the Sultan of Zanzibar presented to Princess Margaret and to the Sultana the insignia of members of the first class of the Order of the Brilliant Star Of Zanzibar, the first occasion on which ladies have been appointed to the Order...'"

"Hurrah," says Mammy tremulously. Her hands, almost translucent, lie a little more calmly on the covers. Without the usual juddering. The waters on the golden beaches of Zanzibar have calmed her ravaged nervous system.

Encouraged, I read aloud another report, from Adelaide.

"'An atomic weapon was successfully exploded at Maralinga late this afternoon... Britain's first groundburst of an atomic weapon.'"

I realize my mistake immediately. Mammy's eyelids flicker. Her attention drifts away. Back into the pain inside. I finish the rest of it quickly.

"'The Chairman of the Australian Safety committee stated the major part of the fall-out occurred a short distance from the firing site. The reddish brown cloud of dust is being tracked by Canberra aircraft and there is no danger of fall-out in pastoral and inhabited areas.'"

"Pass me my rosary beads, please, Pop." Mammy says quietly. She decided to be baptised a Catholic at the start of her illness.

"To be like you and Cecil..."

The priest comes to the house to give her Baptism. The ceremony is over in a few minutes. The shock of the cold water running over Mammy's thinning hair makes her gasp. The skin of her scalp suddenly shows through looking like alabaster. It makes me want to weep. I do not think God would want anyone to have a shock like that. When they are ill. When Mammy herself has so little breath left to spare. Still it is her wish. She is at peace afterwards. Helped by the knowledge that she has done the right thing.

I think that sense of peace helped her drift away. As if dying

146

became an afterthought. Hardly noticeable when the time came. Nothing to get worked up about.

After that, it is hard to cope. So many practical arrangements. To get her buried in Cardiff.

The Parish Priest, Father O'Toole, introduces the Requiem Mass with many kind and comforting words. I sit in a front bench. An arm's length from Mammy's coffin in the centre aisle. I am determined to stay with her through her last journey. At her side all the way. The poignancy and pain is almost unbearable. So little time since we knelt together in Chester Cathedral.

The service is just in its stride when the priest launches into a long Latin dirge. His thunderous tones boom around the church. Fire and brimstone threaten to break right through the solid doors at the main entrance. Froth seeps out from the corners of the priest's mouth. As when a horse bites hard on the bit. Spume and flecked spittle bedeck his robes. His thin lips work the Latin words into a dreadful rhythm. I think of Mammy lying there. This, for her. I am glad she cannot hear it. I read the English translation. Take it for her.

'The day of wrath,
That dreadful day,
Shall the whole world in ashes lay...
What horror must invade the mind,
When the approaching Judge shall find
Few venial faults in all Mankind!

..From that insatiate abyss,
Where flames devour and serpents hiss,
Deliver me, and raise to bliss.'

At the cemetery, I am determined to make it to the graveside. I put my best foot forward. See her safely enfolded. Holy water is sprinkled over Mammy's coffin by the priest. None of it means a thing. She is gone. Gone from me. But not lost. Asleep. Tired. Sleeping so peacefully. I hold her in my heart.

Cecil comes into my bedroom. Looks at me enquiringly.

"Need to use me chamber pot, son. Urgently."

"W.C. best."

"No... Wouldn't make it. Legs... No strength in the legs."

Cecil looks uncertainly around the room.

"Pot's in hat box... Under bed."

Cecil bends down. Leans one hand on the bed. Quickly takes his hand away. Wipes it on the carpet. The mattress is wet. I must have pissed the bed in my sleep.

"What's this?" Cecil is holding up the plaque Dermot gave me. The one carved in wood. He reads it aloud in a puzzled tone of voice.

"'MacDonagh and MacBride
And Connolly and Pearse
Now and in time to be,
Wherever green is worn,
Are changed, changed utterly;
A terrible beauty is born.'"

He turns his nose up. Places the plaque carefully back in the hatbox without comment. The ammonia fumes in the room are overpowering.

"That fellow from the Saint Vincent de Paul's Society gave it me... I can't remember who he is... the pot's in the other hatbox, son. Please, quickly."

Cecil opens the other box. Helps me to sit up. Holds the pot for me. Not many sons would do this. That feels better. Cecil places the full pot down on the carpet. Rushes from the room. I hear him retching in the toilet. A minute later, he pops his head around the door.

"Noreen's gone to ask Doctor MacBride to take a look at you. He knows best..."

Mammy is keeping me company on the sofa. Looking across at me. Smiling encouragement. Her face expands. Then shrinks to a minute speck. The whole room revolves slowly. Ma

O'Keefe's face appears at my first floor bay window. First at one pane, then the next. Goldfish mouth opening and closing.

"Knows best... knows best... knows best... knows best..." She repeats. Eerie, echo-chamber sounds.

Cecil and Noreen hover in the background when the Doctor arrives. Doctor MacBride looks me over. Asks a few questions. Tells Cecil his diagnosis.

"Raging thirst. Weakness of gait. Dizziness. The confusion. Almost certainly diabetes. Don't like the look of that leg either. Wouldn't want to lose it. Needs careful watching. If gangrene set in... need amputating straightaway. Let's get him in hospital today. Get the consultant to take a peep at him."

It is a big hospital. The Cardiff Royal Infirmary. Do everything for you there. Set me up with a bottle to save me getting out of bed right from the start. Even put headphones on me so I can hear a bit of The Archers.

After The Archers, a priest comes to me bedside. Says Cecil has rung him. Has told him how very poorly I am.

"You'll be wanting the Last Rites, Mr Kenealy?"

"Connolly's me name."

"Sorry. Kenealy's probably the collapsed lungs." He looks at a list.

"Ah, yes. There he is. Ward 7." He glances at his watch.

"By rights it should be Father O'Toole seeing to you. From your son's parish. But I am told he is at a symposium... a symposium. Whatever that is. Would y'believe it?"

"No, thanks."

"No, thanks, what, my son?"

"No Last Rites. No sacrament for the dying for me. Thanks."

"I would strongly advise it." He gives an impression he has something important to say on the matter.

"You would?"

"At last anointing, or 'extreme unction' as it is also called, we pray that the Lord will forgive whatever sins you have committed by the senses of sight, hearing, smell, taste, speech, and touch. Thorough isn't it? Covers just about everything." I do not like the little laugh at the end of his speech. But I cannot get out of bed and he is not going away.

"It often helps people to get better too."

"It does?"

"Surely you'd want to meet God, your Judge, with your kettle scraped completely clean, would you not?"

"I'm not sure I'm ready to meet him at all yet, Father."

"Mr Kenealy..."

"Connolly..."

"Sorry. He's Ward 7, isn't he?"

"Collapsed lungs..."

"Mr Connolly. It would be a false mercy if I hid from you the fact that you could soon meet your Maker."

"How's that?" All of a sudden I am all ears.

"Well, on this ward... it's usually..."

"Curtains?"

"People who are very seriously ill."

My state of senile confusion causes me to ask the man to leave without further ado.

I could change my mind, of course. Later. If necessary. If I start to panic. Maybe ask Father O'Toole to call in after his symposium? I do not think I will. I will try to hang on for the time being. Take each moment as it comes.

They have given me all sorts of tablets and injections. I drift deliciously in and out of sleep. Next time I wake, Mrs O'Brien is leaning over me. Dabbing my brow with a damp handkerchief.

"Sean called. Told me they had brought you in."

"How nice of you to come and pay a visit, Mrs O'Brien."

"No need to stand up, Mr Connolly. You stay there. Look, I've brought you a little fortification."

Mrs O'Brien surreptitiously reveals a half bottle of Jameson's whisky in her bag. She unscrews the lid with a practised twist. Soaks her handkerchief in whisky. Presses it against my lips. Nectar of the gods. I am a new man. I become more aware of my surroundings. Notice upward pressure coming from beneath my mattress. Paddy is along for the trip too. A nurse spots him as he is sniffing my saline drip stand. I watch her set out in our direction. There will not be much time.

"Mrs O'Brien, I have been wondering..."

There is so much I want to say.

"Now, don't tire yourself, Mr Connolly."

"I couldn't be tired with you beside me... Listen to me, now... How would it be if I...?"

"Ssshhh..."

That whisky has given me a bit of courage.

"Would y'ever consider taking a lodger in, Mrs O'Brien?"

"Mr Connolly...!"

I cannot tell whether she is shocked or not but she is fondling Paddy's ears with a will.

"Say you will, Mrs O'Brien. Oh, say you will. You'd make a dying man very happy."

"You get yourself better, first, sir. Then... maybe I'll consider it..."

"I'm getting better already, Ma'am. This is marvellous. Recuperating fast and as determined as Robert Bruce's spider. All arms and legs... Haha..." I lunge in Mrs O'Brien's direction to give her a quick cuddle. Succeed only in tearing the saline drip needle out of my arm.

"No dogs." The nurse stares fiercely at Paddy. Fixes the needle back in my arm. Mrs O'Brien never lets things unsettle her.

"I couldn't leave him, you see." She smiles sweetly at the nurse.

"I'll be back in tomorrow, Mr Connolly."

The heads of all the men in the ward turn to follow their progress, as Mrs O'Brien and Paddy pass. They cannot all be interested in golden retrievers. Electricity crackles in the air around her. Mrs O'Brien has a bit of life in her all right.

I go out like a light. What with the excitement of talking to Mrs O'Brien and the whisky. Then wake with a start. Drowse off again. I love drowsiness. Slipping in and out of the brightness of waking, the shadows of sleep. Tracts of Lucretius drift through my mind. I have time to enjoy the thoroughness of his ingenious explanations for the phenomena which surround us. His ideas drift through my mind in wakefulness and deep slumber.

I watch a nurse's shadow flit across the floor. I hear Lucretius explaining to me. 'Our shadow in the sunlight seems to us to move and keep step with us and imitate our gestures, incredible

151

though it is that unillumined air should walk about in conformity with a man's or a woman's movements and gestures. For what we commonly call a shadow can be nothing but air deprived of light. Actually the earth is robbed of sunlight in a definite succession of places wherever it is obstructed by us in our progression, and the part we have left is correspondingly replenished with it. That is why the successive shadows of our body seem to be the same shadow following us along steadily step by step. New particles of radiance are always streaming down and their predecessors are consumed, as the saying goes, like wool being spun into the fire. So the earth is easily robbed of light and is correspondingly replenished and washes off the black stains of shadow.'

I gaze at the sunlight blazing like Venus at the bottom of my water jug. Dazzled. I close my eyes. The water traps the sunlight. It still shines beneath my eyelids. Lucretius expounds in his careful way. 'We do not admit that the eyes are in any way deluded. It is their function to see where light is, and where shadow. But whether one light is the same as another, and whether the shadow that was here is moving over there, or whether on the other hand what really happens is what I have just described – that is something to be discerned by the reasoning power of the mind. A ship in which we are sailing is on the move, though it seems to stand still. Another that rides at anchor gives the impression of sailing by. Hills and plains appear to be drifting astern when our ship soars past them with sails for wings. Mountains rising from the sea in the far distance, though there may be ample space between them for the free passage of a fleet, look as if linked together in a single island.'

Around my bed, faces emerge through clouds of sleep. Cecil is checking my temperature chart. Noreen is filling the fruit bowl with grapes and some dried prunes, just in case. Sean is skating on the highly polished floor.

"Good news, Pop." Noreen's face is flushed. She has been rushing.

"Mmmm...?"

"You are so ill, they have agreed to make a telephone link to Ireland. Your brother, Declan, was desperate to talk to you before... anything happened."

"How did he..?"

"Cecil rang him earlier." I cannot believe the kindness of it. They could not have done anything better.

A nurse wheels a portable telephone to the side of the bed. Lips like a little cupid.

"Thank you, nurse," I say, feeling important.

Cecil passes me the handset. Noreen plumps up the pillows behind my head. Crackling down the line. Then Declan's voice, clear as if he is in the room here with us.

"Connolly, here." He has a surprisingly thick Irish brogue on him.

"Connolly, here too."

"Wha'? Is tha'm'brother speaking? In Cardiff?"

"It is."

"Well, I don't know. How wonderful. How are y'keeping?"

"Oh, just fine... Well. Not too good today. But apart from that..."

"Look here, now. We're all prayin' f'y' over here. Stormin' the heavens as never before. Just get well... will y'?"

"I'll do me best, Declan."

"Mary sends y'all her love. She's real lookin' forwards to meetin' yis."

"Would I remember Mary from the old days at all?"

"Sure, no. She's from Armagh. Mary Cottingham originally. A good Protestant girl... She loves it here now though."

"Ah, good... good to hear about the farm in your letter. Great news."

"We hope t'be seein' yis in the school holidays then. No excuses now... Take plenty of rest... God bless y'."

"Goodbye, Declan. Thanks for calling..."

All of a sudden I am weak. So near and yet so far. I do not think I will make it to see Declan and Mary. But to have spoken to him on the telephone, in person. After all these years. It is too much to comprehend. I look up at Cecil and Noreen. Eyes brimming over with tears of gratitude. They are all so kind to me. Trying to make my last days happy ones.

"See you at visiting time, Pop." The family leave, lingeringly. Fond looks and waves over their shoulders. Reassuring waves because they are worried about me. Think I may not be here when they come back. I am alone. They cannot stay with me every minute of the day. They have lives to lead. Let them go then. Let me lie. The afternoon stretching ahead. An azure sky. Visible through the window opposite my bed. I have my thoughts. My dreams.

I picture Cecil, Noreen and Sean on the deck of a ferry bound for Rosslare. The sun freshly risen in the sky. Waves sparkling. Ignoring the blustery wind. Eager for their first sight of land. Me resting on a life raft. Hand on me hat. Looking after their bags.

Then little Sean swimming in the River Barrow. A warm summer's afternoon. His cousins, Colum and Francis, pulling strongly beside him. Their other cousins running, waving, tumbling on the bank.

Back in Cardiff, I imagine Declan and as many of the family as we can fit around the table at 206, Marlborough Hill, tucking into one of Noreen's dinners. Having a good chin-wag. Declan sipping Cecil's Spanish Sauternes, "A nice drop of stuff tha', Cecil." A sing-song into the early hours.

The last picture before falling asleep. Mammy. The light of my life. I picture her at the table with us. Talking to the children. Ruffling their hair affectionately. Complimenting Noreen on the tenderness of the lamb, the crispness of the meringue atop the lemon meringue pie. Asking Cecil about current affairs. Showing interest in his car's petrol consumption. Chiding me gently when I talk too much.

"Mr Connolly?" A peremptory inquiry. An officer perhaps? No. It is Mr Healey, the consultant.

"Yes. I am Connolly."

"Dr MacBride's patient?"

"Yes."

I wish Cecil and Noreen were here. I feel so helpless. Mr Healey whisks through an examination of me. Rasps out his findings to the Ward Sister who notes them down. His examination is complete. He turns to the Ward Sister and his assembled entourage.

"Dr MacBride's been a bit quick off the mark, as usual. The man's a terrible worrier."

He looks me in the eye for the first time.

"I expect you've been a bit worried yourself, have you, Mr Connolly?"

"Well, yes. I have a bit, sir."

"No need to call me 'sir'. Mr Healey will do."

"Yes, Mr..."

"Right. Start you off on a controlled diet. As of now. Should do the trick. Stabilise you. If not, insulin. The leg's fine. Grazed. Bump into furniture sometimes, do you?"

"Yes, Mr Healey."

"As for the rest of your health, Mr Connolly, you have the constitution of a stallion. You're going to live for years... probably live to be a hundred! Heart and lungs like an ox – if you'll excuse the similes. Hahaha. Haven't heard a heart thumping so well for ages..."

Mr Healey disappears in a swirl of white coats and starched skirts. Alone again. For once, my brain is at a standstill. I have been given the gift of life. How to begin again? How use this gift? I begin to see it. I shall wear my white flannel trousers. Will walk with Mrs O'Brien to our bench in the park. Listen to the children singing. I think they will sing for me. For us.

THE END

Acknowledgements

Permission to quote from the following sources is gratefully acknowledged:

from *The Times*: *Farming Notes and Comments* © The Times Newspapers Limited, London Monday June 3rd 1957; *Prison Workshops Rule Relaxed; Talking Permitted* and *Farm Workers Pay Claim; Three Main Points* © The Times Newspapers Limited, London Tuesday June 4th 1957; *Britain's First Ground Burst* and *Satisfactory Weather* © The Times Newspapers Limited, London Friday October 5th 1956; *"Magical Quality" Of Isle Of Cloves* and *Sultan's Award* © The Times Newspapers Limited, London Saturday October 6th 1956

Approximately 370 words (pp 88, 104-5, 105) from *On the Nature of the Universe* by Lucretius translated by R.E. Latham (Penguin Classics, 1951, Revised Edition, 1994) Translation copyright 1951 by R.E. Latham. Reproduced by permission of Penguin Books Ltd

for quotations from 'Easter 1916' (pp 45-46, 149), 'The Lamentation of the Old Pensioner' (pp 104-105), 'To an Isle in The Water' (p 105), and for 'Down by the Salley Gardens' (p 103) and 'A Drinking Song' (p 137) from *W.B. Yeats: The Poems* (Dent, 1994) A.P. Watt Ltd on behalf of Michael B. Yeats

for the title of the book, from 'A Refusal to Mourn the Death, By Fire, of a Child in London', by Dylan Thomas (*Collected Poems*, Dent) David Higham Associates

About the Author

Born in Cardiff, Patrick Corcoran was educated at Atlantic College, St. Donats, and at Bristol University. His work has been broadcast on Radio 4. This is his first novel. He has won several prizes for his short stories, and was a finalist in *The Daily Telegraph* short story competition. He works as a probation officer, and is married with three children.